T0110796

YUKIO MISHIMA
Thirst for Love

Yukio Mishima wrote countless short stories and thirty-three plays, in some of which he acted. Several films have been made from his novels, including *The Sound of Waves; The Sailor Who Fell from Grace with the Sea;* and *Enjo*, which was based on *The Temple of the Golden Pavilion*. Among his other works are the short-story collections *Death in Midsummer* and *Acts of Worship* and the novels of *The Sea of Fertility* tetralogy. After Mishima conceived the idea of *The Sea of Fertility* in 1964, he frequently said he would die when it was completed. On November 25, 1970, the day he finished *The Decay of the Angel*, the last novel of the cycle, Mishima committed *seppuku* (ritual suicide) at the age of 45.

BOOKS BY YUKIO MISHIMA

Confessions of a Mask

Thirst for Love

Forbidden Colors

The Sailor Who Fell from Grace with the Sea

After the Banquet

The Temple of the Golden Pavilion

Five Modern Nō Plays

The Sound of Waves

Death in Midsummer

Acts of Worship

The Sea of Fertility, A CYCLE OF FOUR NOVELS:

Spring Snow

Runaway Horses

The Temple of Dawn

The Decay of the Angel

Thirst for Love

Thirst for Love

YUKIO MISHIMA

TRANSLATED FROM THE JAPANESE BY

Alfred H. Marks

Vintage International

VINTAGE BOOKS

A DIVISION OF RANDOM HOUSE, INC.

NEW YORK

FIRST VINTAGE INTERNATIONAL EDITION, MARCH 1999

 Published in the United States by Vintage Books, a division of Random House, Inc., New York, and simultaneously in Canada by Random House of Canada Limited, Toronto. Originally published in Japanese as *Ai No Kawaki* by Shinchosha. Copyright 1950 by Yukio Mishima. This translation first published in hardcover in the United States by Alfred A. Knopf, Inc., New York, in 1969.

Library of Congress Cataloging-in-Publication Data

Mishima, Yukio, 1925-1970.
[Ai no kawaki. English]
Thirst for love / Yukio Mishima ; translated from the Japanese by Alfred H. Marks.
p. cm.
ISBN 978-0-375-70507-6
I. Marks, Alfred H. II. Title.
PL833.I7A713 1999
895.6'35—dc21 98-41724
CIP

www.randomhouse.com

147468846

Thirst for Love

1

THAT DAY Etsuko went to the Hankyu department store and bought two pairs of wool socks. One pair was blue, the other brown. They were plain socks, of solid color.

She had come all the way into Osaka and completed her shopping at the Hankyu store at the last station, and now all she was going to do was turn around, board her train, and go home. She wasn't going to a movie. She wasn't even going to have tea, much less a meal. Etsuko hated nothing so much as crowded streets.

If she wanted to go anywhere, all she had to do was go downstairs into the Umeda terminal and take the subway to Shinsaibashi or Dotonbori. Yet if she stepped outside the store and crossed the intersection, where the shoeshine boys were lined up and calling, "Shine! Shine!", she would find herself on the beach of the metropolis, where the rich tides ran.

For Etsuko—born and brought up in Tokyo—Osaka

held inexplicable terrors. City of merchant princes, hoboes, industrialists, stockbrokers, whores, opium pushers, white-collar workers, punks, bankers, provincial officials, aldermen, Gidayu reciters, kept women, penny-pinching wives, newspaper reporters, music hall entertainers, bar girls, shoeshine boys—it was not really this that Etsuko feared. Might it have been nothing but life itself? Life—this limitless, complex sea, filled with assorted flotsam, brimming with capricious, violent, and yet eternally transparent blues and greens.

Etsuko opened her cloth shopping bag and thrust the socks deep within it. A flash of lightning brightened the open windows. It was followed by solemn thunder that made the glass shelves in the store shudder faintly.

The wind bowled in and knocked over a little sign that said "Specials." Clerks ran to close the windows. The store grew dark. The lights, which were kept on even in the daytime, suddenly seemed to glow brighter. There still wasn't any rain.

Etsuko passed her hand through the handle of her shopping bag. The curving bamboo scraped down across her forearm as she lifted her hands to her face. Her cheeks were very warm. That was a common occurrence with her. There wasn't any reason for it; of course, it wasn't a symptom of any illness—it was just that suddenly her cheeks would start to burn. Her hands, delicate though they were, were callused and tanned, and because of that very delicacy seemed rougher. They scratched her cheeks and intensified the burning.

She suddenly felt she could do anything. She could cross that intersection, as if walking out on a springboard, and plunge into the middle of those streets. As she reflected and her gaze was caught by the masses of people moving there on the selling floor among multitudes of things, she momentarily slid into a reverie. Her dreams knew only happy things; misfortune frightened her.

What had given her this courage? The thunder? The two pairs of socks she had just purchased? Etsuko cut through the crowd and hurried to the stairway. She moved with the traffic down to the second floor. Then she approached the Hankyu ticket offices on the first floor.

She looked outside. In the minute or two since it began, the rain had turned to a downpour. The sidewalks were already soaked as if it had been pouring for hours. The rain bounced as it struck.

Etsuko approached one of the exits. Her calm returned. She relaxed as she moved, tired, slightly dizzy. She had no umbrella. She couldn't go out. No, not that. It was no longer necessary that she do so.

She stood by the door and squinted at the row of shops on the other side, beyond the trolley tracks, the traffic signals, and the streetcars so quickly swallowed up by the rain. The rain dashed in even to where she was, dampening her skirt. The doorway area was quite noisy. A man ran up shielding his head under a small valise. A woman dressed in Western clothing hurried in with a scarf covering her hair. It was almost as if they had come to be with Etsuko, who was the only one not soaked.

All around her were men and women who looked as if they could be office workers, all drenched by the rain. They griped, they joked, they looked back rather triumphantly at the rain they had just dashed through. For a time they all turned silent faces toward the rain-filled sky, Etsuko's dry face among all these wet ones.

From some preposterously high place, the rain fell full tilt toward these faces. It seemed to be under tight control. The thunder was receding in the distance, but the sound of the rain numbed the ears, numbed the heart. Even the occasional rending sound of the horns of the passing cars and the gravelly screams of the station loudspeaker could not compete with the tumult of the rain.

Etsuko left the group waiting for the rain to stop and joined one of the long, silent lines at the ticket windows.

The Okamachi station on the Hankyu-Takarazuka line was thirty or forty minutes away from the central Umeda terminal. Expresses did not stop there. Maidemmura, where Etsuko lived, was a suburb of the city of Toyonaka, which had doubled its population after the war. It had become a refuge for many made homeless by the Osaka fire bombings. Other settlers were attracted to the city by the government housing built there. Maidemmura was in Osaka prefecture. In a strict sense it was not rural at all.

Nevertheless, if one wanted to purchase something special, or cheap, he had to take an hour or so and go into Osaka. Etsuko had come shopping on this day before the Autumnal Equinox in order to buy a pomelo to offer before the tablet of her deceased husband, who had loved that fruit. Unfortunately the department store was sold out of pomelos. She didn't want to go outside the store, but driven by conscience or some other obscure impulse, she was about to venture out on the street when the rain stopped her. That was all. Nothing more was necessary.

• • •

Etsuko boarded the local train to Takarazuka and sat down. The rain outside the windows seemed as if it would never stop. The smell of printer's ink on the evening newspaper spread out in front of her by a standing passenger woke her out of her reverie. She looked furtively around her. There was nothing to see.

The trainman's whistle shrilled. The train shook with a deep sound like that of heavy chains gnashing against each other and started rolling. It would repeat the same monotonous maneuver many times over as it advanced hesitantly from station to station.

The rain stopped. Etsuko turned and looked at the way the sunlight was streaming through a rift in the clouds. It came to rest on the residential streets of suburban Osaka like an extended, powerless, white hand.

Etsuko walked as if she were pregnant. It was an ostentatiously indolent walk. She didn't realize it; she had no one who might see it and set her right; but like the slip of paper that a mischievous boy has surreptitiously affixed to a friend's back, that walk was her involuntary sign and seal.

She left the Okamachi station, passed through the *torii* of the Hachiman shrine and the assorted bustlings of small-town streets, and finally came to where the houses were not so frequent. So leisurely was her pace that night had overtaken her.

Lights were burning in the rows of government housing. There were hundreds of units—of the same style, the same life, the same smallness, the same poverty. The road through this squalid community afforded a shortcut that she never took.

These rooms into which one could see so plainly, each with its cheap tea cabinet, its low table, its radio, its muslin floor pillows, its slim fare, of which one could see at times every scrap, and all that steam! Every one of them made Etsuko angry. Her heart had not developed to the point where she could look at poverty, or imagine anything but happiness.

The road darkened. The insects began to sing. The puddles here and there reflected the light of the dying evening. On either side lay ricefields, their surfaces alternately light and dark in the mild damp breeze.

She traversed a meaningless, tedious road of the kind country areas are given to, from which she struck off onto a path that wound near a little stream. She was now in Maidemmura.

Between the stream and the path ran a bamboo thicket, a break in which led to a bridge across the stream. Etsuko crossed the bridge, which was of wood, passed in front of the former tenant farmer's home and through a grove of *kaede* and assorted fruit trees, mounted a curving stone stairway bordered by tea plants, and opened the side door of the Sugimoto home. It was at first glance sumptuous, although the builder had contrived to use cheap lumber in places where it did not show. From the back room issued the laughter of Asako's children. Asako was Etsuko's sister-in-law.

Those children are always laughing. What in the world do they find to laugh at? If there's anything I can't stand it's arrogant laughter like that! Etsuko's thoughts had no particular purpose. She placed her shopping bag on the doorstep.

* * * *

Yakichi Sugimoto had bought this property, of about ten acres, in 1934, five years before he retired from the Kansai Merchant Ships Corporation.

He was originally from the Tokyo area, the son of a tenant farmer, and had worked his way through college. After graduation he was hired by Kansai Ships and assigned to their Osaka home office, in Dojima. He married a girl from Tokyo, and although he lived in Osaka he had his three sons educated in Tokyo. In 1934 he became general manager; in 1938, president. The next year he retired.

When he and his wife happened to visit the grave of an old friend in the Hattori Garden of Souls, a new government cemetery, he was taken with the rolling beauty of the surrounding area. When he inquired about the place, he heard for the first time the name Maidemmura. He selected a sloping site covered with chestnuts and bamboo and graced with orchards, and in 1935 built a simple villa there. At the same time he turned over the cultivation of the fruit trees to a gardener.

This was not at all, however, what his wife and sons had been thinking of as a likely base for leisurely villa life; in fact, it became nothing more than the spot to which Yakichi could drive with his family from Osaka and spend the weekend enjoying the sun and indulging a penchant for farming. Yakichi's languid dilettante of an eldest son, Kensuke, opposed his energetic father's whim with all the force he could muster; but although he loathed it all from the very depths of his heart, he finally found himself—reluctantly, as usual—being coerced into joining his brothers as a farmer.

Among the Osaka men of affairs at this time there were many who loved the soil, and out of the inborn miserliness and sunny pessimism that went with their Kyoto–Osaka area vitality, they looked askance at the villas in the sought-after shore and hot springs areas, and built cottages in the mountains, where land and socializing cost little.

After Yakichi Sugimoto retired, Maidemmura became the hub of his life. The name may well be derived from *mai*, meaning rice, and *den*, meaning field, with the *mura*, of course, meaning village. The area was evidently under the sea in prehistoric times, and as a result the soil was extremely rich. On this ten acres of land Yakichi was able to grow various fruits and vegetables. The tenant farmer and his family, along with three gardeners, were of much help to this tiller of the soil, and after a few years the Sugimoto peaches became greatly prized in the urban markets.

During the war Yakichi lived a life disdainful of the hostilities. It was, however, a unique form of disdain. The city folk, as he saw it, had to buy the bad rations and high-priced black-market rice because they lacked foresight. He, however, had foresight and was able to live a life of composed self-sufficiency. He traced everything back to the doctrine of foresight. Even his retirement at the mandatory age seemed somehow planned. The malaise and boredom other retired executives suffered, so much like the malaise and boredom of imprisonment, he seemed somehow to have missed.

He mocked the military with the half-jesting jibes of a man who holds no grudge. Those jibes hit their highest point when his wife died after coming down with pneumonia, for which she had received a drug newly developed by the medical corps. Yakichi had secured the drug from a friend in the Osaka army headquarters. The drug had no beneficial effect, said Yakichi, save the death of her.

He weeded; he tilled. The peasant blood revived in him; his love of the soil became a fever. Now that neither his wife nor society was watching him, he even went so far as to blow his nose between his fingers. From the very depths of his aging physique, beaten down by suspenders and vests graced with gold chains, emerged intimations of the sturdy frame of a farmer. Beneath his once overly groomed features, the farmer's face came to light. If his subordinates could see him now they would know that the furious brows and glaring eyes that had once terrorized them were features usually associated with old farmers.

It was as if Yakichi were owning land for the first time. Before this he had been able to own building sites. This farm, in fact, had seemed to him only another such piece of property. But now it had come to be *land*. The instinct which held that the concept of ownership has no meaning unless the object owned is land came to live again in him. It seemed as if for the first time the achievements of his life were firm and palpable to hand and heart. It now seemed that the disdain in which he as a rising young man held his father and his grandfather was entirely attributable to their failure to possess so much as one acre of land. Out of a love that was more like a thirst for revenge, Yakichi erected a ridiculously expensive monument to his ancestors at the family temple. He did not dream that Ryosuke would be the first one buried there. For that purpose he might as well have taken a plot at the Hattori Garden of Souls.

On their infrequent visits to the Osaka area, his sons were

puzzled by the changes taking place in their father. The image of him held by Kensuke, the eldest; Ryosuke, the second son; and Yusuke, the youngest, was more or less the image produced by their dead mother's careful nurture. She, brought up in the abominable ways of the Tokyo middle class, permitted her husband to act only as an upper-class executive should. Until she died her husband could not blow his nose with his hand, pick his nose in company, slurp his soup, or hawk and spit into the charcoal fire in the *hibachi*—bad habits that society, in all its magnanimity, tolerates in great men.

The transformation of Yakichi was in his sons' eyes somehow pitiable, foolish, makeshift. It was as if the high spirit of his days as general manager of Kansai Merchant Ships had returned, though now with the businesslike flexibility gone, leaving only the self-made man at his worst. His voice was like that of a farmer running after garden thieves.

Yakichi's bronze bust graced a drawing room that must have been twenty mats in size. His portrait in oil, by one of the shining lights of the Kansai art world, hung there. This bust, this portrait were of the same tradition as the pictures of successive presidents one sees lined up in the voluminous handouts printed for the fiftieth anniversaries of Imperial Japanese So-and-so Corporations. What his sons saw as pitiable was the gratuitous obduracy, the ostentatious pride of the bust enduring unchanged within this old peasant. The remarks he made about the military had behind them the grimy arrogance of the country demagogue. The innocent villagers took his words as evidence of his patriotism, and accorded him even greater respect.

It was ironic that the eldest son, Kensuke, who considered Yakichi impossible, should have been the first to move in with the father. He knew that although his chronic asthma permitted him to live in idleness and escape the draft, it did not exempt him from voluntary service—a duty he took the initiative of choosing by having his father secure him a post with the Maidemmura post office. He moved in with his wife in tow, and it seemed certain that some kind of friction would develop, but Kensuke slid out from under his proud father's absolute power with ease. In this feat his talent for cynicism served him well.

As the war got worse all three of the gardeners were called up, but one of them, a youth from Hiroshima prefecture, managed to have his younger brother, just out of grade school, take his place. That boy, named Saburo, was being brought up in the Tenri sect; for the big festivals in April and October he would leave to meet his mother and, dressed in a white happy coat with the word *Tenri* on the back, would go to worship at the Mother Temple.

* * * *

Etsuko placed her shopping bag on the doorstep as if she were listening to determine what sound it made; then she peered into the dark room. The child's laughter went on and on. Now that Etsuko could hear more clearly she realized the child was not laughing, but crying, rocking himself in the darkness of the deserted room. Asako seemed to have put him down while she cooked. She was the wife of Yusuke, who had not yet returned from Siberia. She had come here with her two children in the spring of 1948, exactly a year before Yakichi asked the widowed Etsuko to join them.

Etsuko started toward her six-mat room, but as she approached it she was surprised to see a light gleaming from above the partition. She did not recall that she had left a light burning.

She opened the sliding door. Yakichi was sitting at the desk engrossed in reading something. He seemed flustered when he looked up and saw his daughter-in-law. Etsuko realized that the red, leather-backed book he had been reading was her diary.

"I'm home," she said, in a clear, cheerful voice. Her look and her reaction to what she had come upon were quite different from what one might have expected. Her voice, her movements were lithe as a maiden's. This husbandless woman was a human being to be reckoned with.

"Welcome home; you're late, aren't you," said Yakichi, who might with more honesty have said: "You're early."

"I'm starved—while I was waiting I borrowed your book." The book he held up was a novel he had substituted for the diary; it was a translated work Kensuke had lent Etsuko. "It was too tough for me; I didn't understand a word."

Yakichi was wearing the old knickerbockers he wore in the fields, a military-style shirt, and an old vest from one of his business suits. His dress was what it had been for a long time, but the almost servile humility with which he comported himself was a tremendous alteration from what he had been during the war, before Etsuko knew him. There was also the decline in his physique, the loss of power in his glance. The once proudly closed lips seemed to have lost the power of coming together; when he spoke, flecks of spittle appeared at the corners of his mouth.

"They were all out of pomelos. I looked all over for them, too, but couldn't find any."

"That's too bad."

Etsuko sank to her knees on the *tatami* and slipped her hand inside her sash. She felt the warmth of her abdomen after the walk; her sash caged the heat like a hothouse. She sensed the perspiration running on her breast. It was a dark, cold sweat, heavy as sweat shed in sleep. It swirled around her, cold though it was, seeming to scent the air.

Her whole body felt constricted by something vaguely discomforting. Then she suddenly slumped to the *tatami.* Someone who did not know her well might have misinterpreted the attitude her body assumed at times like this. Yakichi had many times mistaken it for seductiveness. It was motivated, however, simply by something that overpowered her when she was extremely tired. At such times, Yakichi had found, it was not wise to make advances.

She kicked off her *tabi.* They were flecked with mud; the soles were soiled a dark gray. Yakichi fumbled for something to say.

Finally he came out with: "They're dirty, aren't they?"

"Yes, the road was very poor."

"It was a hard rain. Did it come down in Osaka too?"

"Yes, while I was shopping in the Hankyu." Etsuko recalled the sound of the rain assaulting her ears. All the world seemed to have changed to rain under that sky tight with storm.

She said nothing more. This room was all she had. She began to change her kimono, heedless of Yakichi's eyes. The electric power was weak, and the bulb was dim. Between the silent Yakichi and the wordlessly moving Etsuko, the only sound was the shriek of silken sash being unwound, like the scream of a living thing.

Yakichi found it impossible to remain silent for long. He

was conscious of Etsuko's unspoken reproach. He said that he would like to eat and made his way to his eight-mat room across the hall.

Etsuko started tying her everyday Nagoya sash and wandered over to the desk. Holding the sash behind her back with one hand, she riffled the pages of the diary with the other. A small, bitter smile passed over her lips.

Father doesn't know this is my false diary. Nobody knows that it is a false diary. Nobody even imagines how well one can lie about the state of one's own heart.

She opened to yesterday's page. She looked down at the page filled with characters and read:

September 21 (Wednesday)

Nothing happened today, all day. The heat wasn't too bad. The garden was full of the noise of insects. In the morning I went to the village distribution center to get our ration of *miso*. The child of the people who run the distribution center has pneumonia but was brought around by penicillin and seems to be mending. It was none of my business, but I was relieved.

When one lives in the country, one has to have a simple soul. Somehow, I have sought this and matured. I'm not bored. Not a bit bored. I'm never bored. I now understand the gentle feeling of breathing easily that comes to a farmer when he doesn't have to be out in the fields. I am wrapped in Father's generous love. I feel as if I am fifteen or sixteen again.

In this world the simple soul, the artless spirit—this alone—is enough. Nothing else is necessary, I believe. In this world only people who can work and stir themselves are necessary. In the swamp of city life, the flood of connivances to which the heart is subject destroys it.

There are calluses on my hands. Father praises me for

them. They are the hands of a true person. I don't get angry anymore; I don't get depressed. That terrible memory, the memory of my husband's death, doesn't bother me so much anymore. Mellowed by the soft burgeoning sun of autumn, my heart has developed magnanimity; I give thanks to everything I see.

I think of S. She is in the same situation as I. She has become the companion of my heart. She, too, lost her husband. When I think of her misfortune, I am consoled. She is a widow of truly beautiful, clean, simple soul, and so she will certainly have opportunities to remarry. I would like to have a long talk with her before that happens, but since Tokyo is a long way from here the opportunity is certainly to be denied me. It would be nice if she sent me at least one letter, but . . .

The initial is the same, but since I've changed him to a woman, nobody will know. The name S comes up too much, but I don't have to worry about that. After all, there's no proof. To me this is a false diary, though no human being can be so honest as to become completely false.

She attempted to analyze what she really had in mind when she first set down these hypocrisies; then she rewrote them in her mind.

Even though I might rewrite them, there is no reason to believe the result says what I really think.

Rationalizing in this way, she recast the diary passage:

September 21 (Wednesday)

Another painful day has ended. How I ever got through this day is a mystery to me. In the morning, I went to the distribution center to get our ration of *miso*. The child of the people who run the distribution center had pneumonia but was brought around by penicillin and seems to be mending. That's too bad! If the child of that woman who goes around talking about me behind my back should die, I would get some consolation, anyway.

When one lives in the country, one has to have a simple soul. Just the same, the Sugimotos, with their rotten, stuck-up effeteness, make country life increasingly more painful. I love the simple soul. I even go so far as to think that there is nothing so beautiful in this world as the simple spirit in the simple body. When, however, I stand before the deep chasm that lies between my soul and that soul, I do not know what to do. Is it possible to transfer the obverse of a coin to the reverse? Simply take a coin with an unbroken surface and make a hole in it. That is suicide.

Every once in while I come close, driven by a decision to lay my life on the line. My partner flees—to some infinitely distant place. And thus, again, I am alone, surrounded by boredom. Those calluses on my fingers—they are ridiculous.

Etsuko went by the creed, nevertheless, that one should never take anything too seriously. One who walks barefoot will end up cutting his feet. To walk one needs shoes, just as to live one needs a ready-made objective. Etsuko turned the pages heedlessly and talked to herself.

Just the same, I am happy. I am happy. Nobody can deny it. In the first place, there is no evidence.

She thumbed ahead in the diary. The white pages went on and on. And so, finally, a year of this happy diary came to an end . . .

Meals in the Sugimoto household followed a peculiar routine. There were four groups: Kensuke and his wife on the second floor, Asako and her children on the first floor, Yakichi and Etsuko in another part of the first floor, and Miyo and Saburo in the servant's quarters. Miyo cooked rice for everyone, but the other dishes were prepared by the group that ate them. Out of Yakichi's willfulness sprang the custom by which the two sons' families were allotted a fixed sum monthly for household expenses and expected to manage within it. Only he, he felt, did not have to conform to so straitened a regimen. His invitation to Etsuko—who had nowhere to turn with her husband dead—was based on nothing but the wish to utilize her services as cook. It was a simple impulse, nothing more.

Yakichi took the best of the fruits and vegetables harvested. Only he had the right to pick the nuts from the Shiba chestnut tree, the most delicious of them all. The other families were forbidden to do so. Only Etsuko shared them with him.

When he arrived at the decision to bestow on Etsuko these perquisites, perhaps a certain ulterior motive was already moving within Yakichi. The best Shiba chestnuts, the best grapes, the best Fuyu persimmons, the best strawberries, the best peaches—the right to share these seemed to Yakichi a privilege for which no compensation was too great.

Thanks to these marks of special favor received by Etsuko so soon after her arrival, she became the object of the jealousy and resentment of the other two families. That jealousy and resentment soon excited a further, vicious surmise, an exceedingly plausible calumny that seemed somehow to reach Yakichi and direct his conduct. Yet the more satisfactory succeeding events were in corroborating the suspicions aroused by the first hypothesis, the more difficult it became for the one who arrived at it to believe what he saw.

Could this woman whose husband was dead less than a

year willingly enter into a physical relationship with her father-in-law? She was still very young, still supremely eligible for marriage; could she have voluntarily set out to bury the last half of her life? How could she benefit by giving herself to this old man, who was over the hill of his sixtieth year? To be sure, she was a woman with no close relatives, but was this something one did nowadays because "one must eat"?

All kinds of conjectures built around Etsuko a wall that excited new curiosity. Inside this wall she came and went, bored, weary, yet with abandon, like a lone running bird.

Kensuke and his wife Chieko were in their second-floor apartment, eating. Chieko had married Kensuke out of sympathy for his cynicism, and since her sympathy had built-in escape hatches, she could now behold her husband's extraordinary shiftlessness and not suffer any disillusionment with married life. This literary youth gone to seed and his literary maid had married by the credo that goes: "Nothing in this world is so stupid as marriage." Yet even now the two could sit, side by side in their bow window, reading aloud the prose poems of Baudelaire.

"Poor Father," said Kensuke, "when you get to his age, your troubles never seem to stop coming. I went by Etsuko's room a while ago and noticed that her light was burning, though I was sure she had gone out. I went in—rather quietly, I suppose—and lo and behold, Father was there absorbed in reading Etsuko's diary. He was so caught up he didn't know I was standing right behind him. Then I said, 'Father,' and he jumped, he was so surprised. He recovered his composure and frowned at me, with the frightful glare that I was always afraid to look at when I was a child. Then he said: 'If you tell Etsuko I've been reading her diary, I'll throw you and your wife out of this house. Do I make myself clear?' "

"I wonder what made him so concerned about Etsuko that he has taken to reading her diary," said Chieko.

"Maybe he's noticed that for some reason or other she's been restless lately, though I don't think he realizes that she has fallen in love with Saburo. That's the way I see it, anyway. Yet she's a shrewd woman, and I don't think she'll expose her heart to a diary."

"I just can't believe what you say about Saburo, but I have great respect for your powers of observation and won't argue with you. Frankly, it's Etsuko I can't figure out. If she could say what she wants to say and do what she wants to do, we could help her."

"There are some things that don't work out as you plan them. And Father has lost all his pride since Etsuko came," said Kensuke.

"His pride's been gone since the land reform."

"I guess you're right. As the son of a tenant farmer, the moment when he told himself, 'I own land,' was a great one. He strutted like a private promoted to corporal. All that people who didn't own land had to do to get it was work thirty or so years for a steamship company and then become head of the firm. That was his odd formula for success. He took delight in tricking the process with talk about working hard and living austerely.

"During the war he had tremendous power. He talked about Tojo as if he were some clever old friend who had made money in stocks. I was just a post office worker, and I used to listen to it humbly. Since he wasn't an absentee landowner, he didn't lose much of his land here in the postwar reform, but when they let a yokel like the tenant farmer Okura become a landowner at a ridiculously low price, it was an awful blow. It was then that he started to say: 'If I had known things would come to this, I wouldn't have worked so hard for sixty years!' To see these swarms of people getting land they hadn't worked for was to him like losing his reason for being. Though you mightn't think so, he really has a lot of the sentimentalist left in him, and he actually seemed to enjoy the idea of being one of the martyrs of that time. If, when he was most depressed, they had charged him with being a war criminal and had escorted him off to Sugamo, he might even have been rejuvenated."

"Etchan is lucky," said Chieko. "She doesn't know how tyrannical Father was. One moment, though, she's happy, and the next moment she's depressed, but—let the matter of Saburo be what it might—I just can't fathom how a woman can, before the period of mourning for her husband is over, become her father-in-law's mistress."

"Just the same," her husband answered, "she's a simple, fragile woman. She's like the willow tree, and never resists the wind, but just blindly clings to her notion of constancy, so much so that she's incapable of noticing when the one she is constant to changes. Blown about in the dusty wind, she didn't notice that the man she clung to because he was her husband had become a different man."

Kensuke was a skeptic who prided himself on an ability to see through mankind as if it were transparent.

Night came, and the three families went on with their separate lives. Asako was involved with her children. She put them to bed early, climbed in with them, and slept.

Kensuke and his wife did not come downstairs. Outside their windows they could see the far slope on which the distant lights of the government housing units were strewn like sand. All there was between here and there was a dark sea of rice fields, along the edge of which the lights looked as if they belonged to a town strung along an island shore. In that town, it seemed, a majestic activity went on endlessly. In that town, one might imagine, a quiet religious conclave was going on, in which motionless men sat immersed in ecstasy and awe. In that rapt silence, one might dream, a calm, endlessly slow murder was being perpetrated in the lamplight—if Etsuko had looked at the lights of the government housing units in this way she would not have been tempted to treat them with scorn.

At times the whistle of the Hankyu train sent its note reverberating over the dark ricefields, like a flock of scrawny night birds flying swiftly with raucous cries. The beating wings of the train whistle set the night air trembling. It was the time of the year when, if one looked up suddenly, one might see a dim, blue-green flash of lightning flicker silently across a corner of the night sky and disappear.

In the evening, after supper, no one came to visit the rooms occupied by Yakichi and Etsuko. There had been a time when Kensuke came by to kill time chattering, or Asako dropped in with the children, or everybody came in to enjoy themselves. By degrees, however, Yakichi's distaste for playing host became clear, and the others began to keep their distance. Yakichi could not stand competing with anyone for Etsuko's time.

In those hours, they were not pressed to do anything.

Sometimes they played *go*, which Yakichi taught her. This was the only opportunity Yakichi had ever had to display his skill as mentor to a young woman. Tonight again they sat at the *go* board.

Lost in the joy of lifting the weight of each *go* stone in her fingers, constantly groping with her hand in the bowl of stones, Etsuko never took her eyes from the board, to which they clung as if possessed. Her attitude seemed to display extraordinary absorption, but in fact she was drawn by nothing more than the meaningless ordering of the regularly intersecting black lines. Yakichi, too, was struck by Etsuko's absorption. Was it in the game or something else? He observed this lone young woman, free of embarrassment, oblivious in the joy of frivolous abstraction, her white teeth faintly visible in her partly opened mouth.

At times her *go* stones struck the board with a high-pitched sound. It was as if they were lashing something, an attacking dog, perhaps. At such times Yakichi would furtively observe his daughter-in-law's face and place his stones gently, as if remonstrating with her.

"What terrific power! Just like the duel between Musashi Miyamoto and Kojiro Sasaki at Ganryushima."

From behind Etsuko came the heavy sounds of steps in the hallway. It wasn't the lightness of a woman's step. It wasn't the gloom-ridden burden of a middle-aged man. It was a feverish, youthful weight that bounced from the soles of the feet and made the boards in the hall, dark in the night, squeak with a noise like a groan, like a shout.

Etsuko's hand paused in the act of setting down a stone. Her fingers seemed to be barely supported by the stone. Yet it was essential that those fingers, trembling in spite of themselves, grip the stone firmly. She feigned that she was carefully considering her next play. It was not, however, a difficult play, and it was important that her father-in-law not be made suspicious by undue hesitation.

The door slid open. Saburo remained kneeling outside and poked his head into the opening. Etsuko heard him say: "Good night, sir."

Yakichi grunted and bent forward to place a stone. Etsuko stared at his stiff, knobby, ugly old fingers. She said nothing to Saburo. She did not look toward the door. It closed. The footsteps retreated in the direction opposite Miyo's bedroom. There, facing west, was Saburo's three-mat room.

2

DOGS *MAKE* country nights unbearable with their howling. The old setter Maggie, tied in the shed in back, lifted her ears at the sound of a pack of wild dogs passing through the orchard and the grove nearby. Then she lifted her voice in a long, stupid howl, as if complaining of her solitary confinement. The wild dogs paused in their rustling passage through the bamboo grass and answered her. Etsuko, a light sleeper, awoke.

She had gone to bed only an hour ago. A long period of sleep was a duty she still owed the ensuing day. She searched her mind for a hope that would justify tomorrow. Any tiny, ordinary hope would suffice. Without that who can live till morning? Some mending that is still to be done, tickets for tomorrow's trip, the small quantity of *saké* left in the bottle to provide tomorrow's liquid sustenance—all these one must offer to the next day before one can face the dawn.

What did Etsuko have to offer? Oh yes, two pairs of

socks, one blue, one brown. Her gift of these to Saburo was all that tomorrow meant to Etsuko. She was not religious, yet like devoutly religious women, Etsuko found in the emptiness of her hopes the purest of meanings. She clung to these frail cords—one blue, one brown. By them she dangled from this impossible, murky, pitch-black, bloated balloon of a tomorrow; and where it would take her she did not think about. Not thinking about things was the basis of Etsuko's contentment. It was her reason for being.

Etsuko's entire body was still swathed in the groping of Yakichi's dry, gnarled fingers. Even an hour or two of sleep had not wiped it off. A woman who has been caressed by a skeleton can never forget that caress. It was a new skin added to her skin—transparent, damp, thinner than the chrysalis a butterfly is about to shed. It was as if she had been painted with an invisible pigment, which if she so much as moved a muscle would fly into luminous shreds in the darkness.

She looked around her with eyes accustomed to the dark. Yakichi, oddly enough, was not snoring. The nape of his neck gleamed faintly like a plucked fowl. The sound of the clock above the shelf chopping time and the chirping of the crickets under the floor placed this night within earthly boundaries, without which it would not have been of this earth—this night that hovered over Etsuko and filled her with fear that she was turning as rigid as a fly dropped in gelatin.

She lifted her head slowly. The mother-of-pearl on the door of the heirloom cabinet glistened blue.

She closed her eyes tightly. The memory of it came back. It had taken place six months earlier, when shortly after she came here she started taking walks alone and was immediately dubbed eccentric by the villagers. Etsuko ignored them and walked on. It was then that they noticed that she walked as if pregnant, from which they deduced that she was a woman with a past.

From a corner of the Sugimoto property, one could look across the creek at the expanse of the Hattori Garden of Souls. Very few people visited the graves there except during the equinoctial holidays. In the afternoons, on the broad slopes of the cemetery, the countless tombstones threw tiny shadows on the ground. From here the cemetery, wavy with undulations and surrounded by hilly woodland, seemed cheerful and pure. At times one could see the sun reflecting off single granules in the white quartz of one or another of the tombs.

Etsuko was particularly fond of the breadth of the sky above the cemetery and the stillness of the broad path that ran through it. This white, bracing tranquillity, mixed with the scent of shrubbery and tender tree shoots, made her feel as at no other time that her spirit was unclothed.

It was the time for gathering herbs. Etsuko walked along the creek collecting horsetail and starwort in her sleeve. In one place the creek water had run over the bank. There was parsley there. The creek flowed under a bridge and then cut past the concrete drive that came from Osaka where it terminated at the cemetery gate. Etsuko circled the round, grassy plot at the entrance and headed for her favorite path. She marveled that this respite had been vouchsafed her. It was like a reprieve.

She passed by some children playing catch. After a time she came to a green plot that as yet bore no monuments. It lay inside the wall that ran along the creek. As she started to sit down, she noticed a boy lying on his back evidently absorbed in the book he held over his face. It was Saburo. He felt her shadow as it hovered over him and sat up.

"Mrs. Sugimoto," he said. At that moment all the starwort and horsetail fell from her sleeve onto his face.

The changes of expression that then rapidly passed over Saburo's face gave Etsuko a cool and distinct sense of joy, of the kind that comes to one who encounters a simple and neatly soluble equation. When the herbs first struck his face, he thought she was teasing him and exaggerated his efforts to escape. Then he looked at Etsuko's expression and realized it had been an accident. His face swiftly sobered and turned apologetic. He stood up. Then he sank down on his knees and helped Etsuko retrieve the spilled starwort.

Then I asked him: "What have you been up to?"

"I've been reading a book, madam."

He blushed and showed her the samurai adventure story. His "madam" made her think of military usage, though this boy only eighteen had not been a soldier. He had been brought up hearing the dialect of Hiroshima and was now testing his use of standard speech.

Saburo volunteered that he had gone to get the bread ration and was relaxing on the way back when Etsuko discovered him. His plea was more ingratiating than defensive. "I won't tell," said Etsuko.

She recalled that she had asked about the damage done to Hiroshima by the atomic bomb. He said that his immediate family lived outside the city proper but that one whole family of his relatives had died in the bombing. There was nothing more for Etsuko and Saburo to say. He did not wish to be so forward as to ask her any questions.

When I first saw Saburo, I thought he must be at least twenty. I can't recall how old he looked when I saw him as he lay on the grass of the Hattori Garden of Souls. He was young. His cotton shirt, which was full of patches, was open, and his sleeves were rolled up. Perhaps he was hiding his badly frayed cuffs. His arms were splendid, arms that city men don't acquire until much later. They were tanned, those well-developed arms; all the golden fuzz on them made them look as if their maturity embarrassed them.

Etsuko could only look at him reprovingly. It wasn't an expression that suited her, but she had no other. She wondered if he knew why. *Of course he didn't. He was conscious only of the presence of another nuisance of a woman come to live with his nuisance of an employer.*

His voice! That slightly nasal, smoky, subdued, yet childish voice! Those words that seemed to be torn one by one from his uncommunicative tongue! How round those words, like plain wild fruit!

Nevertheless, when Etsuko saw him the next day she was able to look at him without being moved in the slightest. No reproof—just a smile.

That's right. Nothing happened.

Then one day when she had been there a month, Yakichi asked Etsuko to mend the old suits he wore for farming. He hurried her to complete the job, and it took her well into the night. At one o'clock in the morning, Yakichi, who should have been asleep, came into Etsuko's room. He praised her diligence, slipped his arms into the jacket that had been repaired, and silently smoked his pipe for a while.

"Do you sleep well now?"

"Yes. It's different from Tokyo—so quiet."

"You're not telling me the truth," said Yakichi.

"Actually I'm not sleeping very well at all," said Etsuko. "It's just too quiet, quieter than I like it."

"That's too bad. I shouldn't have brought you away." Yakichi's reply had in it a touch of front-office sarcasm.

Even when Etsuko accepted Yakichi's invitation to come to Maidemmura, she anticipated the occurrence of nights like this. In fact she rather welcomed them. Earlier she had wished to die with her husband—the death of an Indian widow. It was an occult thing, that sacrificial death she dreamed of, a suicide proffered not so much in mourning for her husband's death as in envy of that death. What she desired was not any common, ordinary death, but a slow death, over a protracted period of time. Was it not that in the depth of her jealousy she sought something that would enable her never to fear jealousy again? Behind this sordid craving, as wretched as a craving for carrion, did there not lurk a fervent desire to have everything for herself—a purposeless greed?

Her husband's death . . . It was a day toward the end of autumn. She could still see clearly the hearse pulled up to the back door of the Hospital for Infectious Diseases. The workmen had lifted the casket. There was the damp smell of incense and mildew and corpses in the basement mortuary, as well as the ghastly presence of the artificial white lotuses thick with gray dust, and the damp *tatami* for overnight mourners, and the couch used as the bier, its leather cover peeling. From this mortuary with its portable shrine —a waiting room in which the tablets of the dead keep changing—the workmen carried the coffin up the sloping concrete ramp. One of the workmen was wearing army shoes, and the hobnails in them struck the concrete with a sound like gnashing teeth. The door opened . . .

Etsuko had never known a sunburst of such profusion, of such emotion, as that which she met in that moment. That flooding sunshine of early November, that transparent geyser filling and overflowing all.

The back door of the hospital opened onto a flat basin of the city once completely devastated by fire bombings. On the other side ran the embankment of the Chuo line, overgrown with withered vegetation. Half the neighborhood was made up of new houses and houses under construction; the rest was still ruins of fire, given over to weeds, rubbish, and assorted debris. The November sunshine spread over everything. The handlebars of bicycles running along the broad avenue that traversed the area shone in it. Even from the rubbish piles in the ruins, bright shards, perhaps from beer bottles, dazzled the eye. The sunlight struck the casket and then Etsuko with the force of a cataract.

The hearse started its engine. Etsuko got in behind the casket in the curtained interior.

What she thought about on the way to the crematorium was neither jealousy nor death. All she pondered was the glare that had just struck her. In her lap her hands toyed with a bouquet of autumn flowers. There were chrysanthemums. There was bush clover. There were Chinese balloon flowers. There were cosmos, wilted from the overnight stay. The front of her mourning dress was sprinkled with yellow pollen.

What did she think in that light-bathed time? Of liberation from jealousy? From the myriad sleepless nights? From her husband's sudden fever? From the Hospital for

Infectious Diseases? From his horrible, delirious ravings in the dead of night? From the awful odors? From death?

Was Etsuko even jealous that this abundant sunshine was a thing of this earth? And was that because jealousy had become the only emotion she could maintain for any length of time?

A feeling of liberation should contain a bracing feeling of negation, in which liberation itself is not negated. In the moment a captive lion steps out of his cage, he possesses a wider world than the lion who has known only the wilds. While he was in captivity, there were only two worlds to him—the world of the cage, and the world outside the cage. Now he is free. He roars. He attacks people. He eats them. Yet he is not satisfied, for there is no third world that is neither the world of the cage nor the world outside the cage. Etsuko, however, had in her heart not the slightest interest in these matters. Her soul knew nothing but affirmation.

She could not help feeling that the sunlight that bathed her there by the back door of the hospital was a shocking waste committed by heaven, now gratuitously inundating the earth. She came to the conclusion later that she was much more comfortable in the half-light of the hearse. Each time the car bumped, something rattled in her husband's coffin. Perhaps it was her husband's pipe, placed with him because he treasured it, knocking against the wooden side. It should have been wrapped in something. Etsuko placed her hand against the white cloth that covered the outside of the casket at the spot the noise was coming from. The pipe, or whatever it was, went silent—as if holding its breath.

She pulled back a corner of the curtain. After a time she saw another hearse ahead of hers slow down and swing from the center of the boulevard into a tasteless mall surrounded by benches and a preposterously large building that looked like a kiln. It was the crematorium.

Etsuko remembered thinking: *I have not come to cremate my husband, but to cremate my jealousy.*

But when her husband's remains were burned, would her jealousy be consumed too? Her jealousy was in a sense a contagion caught from her husband. It had attacked her body, her nerves, her bones. If she wished to burn her jealousy, she must walk with her husband's coffin into the innermost depths of that blast furnace of a building. There was no other way.

For three days before he took sick, her husband had not come home. He went to work. He was not one to be so carried away by a love affair that he took a day off from the office. He simply could not bear to come home, where Etsuko was waiting. She went to the neighborhood public phone five times a day but hesitated about calling. Yet when she did call he always came to the phone. He was never brutal to her then. His soft, sweet, purring excuses, however, and his deliberate lapses into lisping Osaka speech reminded Etsuko of the way he would twist out his cigarettes in the ashtray and intensify her pain. She preferred abuse. Although at first glance he was a big man to whose lips abuse might spring readily, Ryosuke could repeat to her in gentle tones promises he had long decided not to fulfill. Etsuko could not combat it. She would have been much better off if she had not called him in the first place.

"It's hard to talk here, but last night I met an old friend.

First he asked me to go play mah-jongg. He's high up in the Commerce Ministry and I couldn't be rude to him. What? Yes, tonight I'm coming home. Right after work, I'm coming home. . . . But I've got mountains of work. . . . Should you get dinner? Do it or don't do it, I don't care—whatever you like. . . . If I've eaten, I'll eat again when I get home. Look, I'm hanging up. Mr. Kawaji here is getting jealous. . . . Yes, I see. I understand. All right, goodbye." Dandy that he was, Ryosuke put on an air of bourgeois contentment among his colleagues.

Etsuko waited. Then she waited some more. He didn't come home. Was it because on the rare evenings that he did spend at home Etsuko never nagged him or called him to account? All she did was look at her husband with sadness in her eyes. Those bitch's eyes, those dumb, sad eyes, made Ryosuke angry. It was the something for which the woman waited, her hands held out like a beggar's. Something for which the woman with eyes more and more like a beggar's waited. For Ryosuke, it sniffed out all the desolate fears of their ugly skeleton of a marital relationship and flensed it of the detail of life.

He turned his solid—more precisely his "stolid"—back and feigned sleep. One night in summer he felt his wife's lips touch his body as he slept, and he slapped her for it. "Don't you have any shame?" he said in a sleepy voice, slapping her. Without emotion, as if he were striking a mosquito that had landed on him.

It started that summer. He began to take pleasure in making his wife's jealousy overflow.

Etsuko noticed that he was acquiring neckties she had not seen before. One morning he called her to him as he stood in front of the full-length mirror and asked her to tie his necktie. Etsuko's fingers shook in joy and anxiety; she couldn't seem to get it tied. Finally it was done. Ryosuke stepped away from her brusquely and asked: "How do you like it? Nice pattern?"

"Oh? I didn't notice. It's new, isn't it? Did you buy it?"

"Come on! You noticed; I can tell."

"Well, it suits you."

"I should say it does."

From the drawer of Ryosuke's desk, a woman's handkerchief protruded—as if he had placed it there deliberately. It reeked of cheap perfume. After that there were things even worse, things that filled the air of the house with a bitter smell. Etsuko put a match to the pictures of a woman he had arranged on his desk and burned them one by one. Her husband had anticipated as much. "Where are my pictures?" he asked when he came home. Etsuko stood before him with arsenic tablets in one hand and a glass of water in the other. He swept the tablets from her hand, and she fell over a mirror stand and cut her forehead.

But, oh, the fervor of her husband's caresses that night! That capricious storm one night long! That ironic caricature of happiness!

The evening that Etsuko resolved to poison herself again her husband came home. Two days later he took sick. Two weeks later he died.

"My head! My head! I can't stand it!" Ryosuke said in the entranceway; he didn't come in.

Etsuko had intended to take poison again when he returned. Now that was thwarted. It looked as if her husband had come home to torture her. This evening she did not feel the joy she usually felt at the return of this husband—a joy that exasperated her with herself. She rested her hand coldly on the sliding door, looked down at her husband sitting unmoving on the step, and felt proud. It was a pride in the success of the wager she had not proposed, with death as the stakes. She did not realize that the idea of death had already flown lightly out of her mind.

"Have you been drinking?" she asked.

Ryosuke shook his head and glanced up at her. He wasn't conscious that in his eyes as he looked up was the same dog's look he loathed, the look his wife always wore. A sluggish, feverish, earnest look—like that of an animal ignorant as to why a disease is developing within itself. It was the earnest, pleading look an animal might turn to its keeper. Perhaps now, for the first time, Ryosuke had an inkling that something inexplicable was happening in his body. He was sick; but sickness is not sickness alone.

The short sixteen days after that were the happiest in Etsuko's life. How alike they were—her honeymoon and her husband's death—those two short periods of joy! Now she traveled with him to death's resort. There was in this trip, as in the wedding journey, the same abuse of body and soul, the same untiring, insatiable desire and pain.

Her husband lay with his chest bare, haunted by feverish nightmares, manipulated by the dexterous puppetry of death, groaning like a bride. In the last days, as his brain was being attacked, he would suddenly sit up as if doing calisthenics, stick out his parched tongue, bare his front teeth dyed terracotta by the blood that oozed from his gums, and laugh out loud.

In their room on the second floor of the Atami Hotel, the morning after the first night, he had laughed like that. He had opened the window and looked down at the gently undulating lawn. There was a family of Germans, guests of the hotel, with a big greyhound dog. The five- or six-year-old son was about to take the dog for a walk. Suddenly the dog saw a cat slinking under the shrubs and took off after her. The boy forgot to let go of the chain and was dragged on his backside across the lawn. Watching this, Ryosuke broke out in a laugh of pure, uninhibited joy. He bared his teeth and roared. Etsuko had never seen him laugh like that.

Etsuko put on her slippers and ran to the window. That morning blaze on the lawn! That bright sea at the edge of the garden so deftly sloped that it seemed to join imperceptibly with the beach. They went down to the lobby. In the letter rack on a pillar were colorful travel booklets under a sign saying: "Help yourself." Ryosuke took one, and while they were waiting for breakfast, he cleverly folded it into a paper airplane. Their table was by a window that looked out on the garden. "Look," he said, and sailed the travel booklet airplane out toward the ocean. How silly!

It was nothing but one of Ryosuke's many tricks to ingratiate and delight the woman he was interested in. At that time, let it be said, he was really interested in pleasing Etsuko. He really wanted to impress this new wife. What sincerity!

She still had some money. Until recently there had been just Etsuko and her father—all that were left of a wealthy old family tracing its lineage back to a famous general of the civil war period. Their fortune lay gathered in a stubbornly defended heap. Then the end of the war, the property tax, her father's death, and Etsuko's inheritance—a shockingly small bundle of securities. At any rate, that morning at the Atami Hotel, the two were a couple in every sense of the word. Ryosuke's fever later made the two one once more. In this cruel joy that unexpectedly came to her again, Etsuko seemed to find the fullest, the most detailed, the greediest, the most wretched of pleasures. Her nursing of her husband was almost enough to make an onlooker avert his eyes.

It took time to diagnose the illness as typhoid. For a long time they thought it was a peculiar, pernicious cold accompanied by catarrh. There was the relentless headache, the sleeplessness, the complete lack of appetite; yet there were no indications of the two characteristic symptoms of early typhoid—the mounting fever and the irregularity of body temperature and pulse. In the first two days, there was the headache and general body lassitude, but not the fever. The day after he came home, he did not go to the office.

All that day, oddly, he passed docilely putting things in order, like a child playing in someone else's house. An amorphous, incomprehensible anxiety arose out of his numbing lethargy. As Etsuko entered his six-mat study bearing him coffee, she found her husband spread-eagled on the *tatami* in his blue and white lounging robe. He was biting his lip as if testing it. The lip wasn't swollen, but it felt as if it was going to be.

When he saw Etsuko, he said: "I don't want any coffee."

She hesitated, and he went on: "Move the knot of my sash toward the front. It's digging into me, and I can't stand it. I'd do it myself, but it's too much trouble."

For a long time now, Ryosuke had not liked Etsuko to

touch him. He didn't even like her to help him put on his coat. What made him act this way today? Etsuko put the coffee tray down on his desk and knelt beside him.

"What are you doing?" he asked. "You remind me of a masseuse." She wedged her hand under his body and slid around the polka-dot sash and its perfunctory knot. He did not attempt to raise his body—his haughty, heavy trunk bearing down on Etsuko's slender hand. It hurt her, but even in her pain she regretted that the task took only a few seconds.

"Rather than lie here like this, wouldn't you like to go to bed? Shall I lay it out?"

"Leave me alone. I feel fine this way."

"How about your temperature? It seems higher than before."

"It's the same as before—normal."

At this time Etsuko dared something that surprised even her. She pressed her lips against her husband's forehead to determine his temperature. Ryosuke said nothing. His eyes moved languidly under his closed eyelids. The greasy, grimy skin of his forehead . . . Yes, it was a forehead that after a time would lose its ability to perspire—typhoid's special effect—and then would dry up and burn like fire. A mad brow, and before long the dirt-colored brow of a corpse.

The next evening Ryosuke's temperature swiftly climbed to 103.4. He complained of low back pain and headache. He moved his head constantly, seeking a cool place on the pillow, and thus smeared his pillow case with hair oil and scurf. That night Etsuko brought out the water pillow. He could take only liquids, and those with difficulty. She pressed apples, put the juice in a feeding cup and gave it to him to drink. The next morning the doctor came and said he had only a cold.

So I saw my husband at last come round to me, come round before my eyes. It was like watching a piece of flotsam wash up before me. I bent over and carefully, minutely, inspected this strange suffering body on the surface of the water. Like a fisherman's wife, I had gone every day to the water's edge. I had lived alone and waited. Thus I finally found, in the sluggish water among the rocks in the bay, this washed-up corpse. It was still breathing. Did I pull it out of the water right away? No, I did not. All I did was, fervently, with passion and effort, without sleep, without rest, bend over the water and stare.

So I watched this still-breathing body, completely immersed in the water, to see if it would groan again, shout again, until finally its hot exhalations died away. I knew: if he were revived, this piece of flotsam would leave me. He would without doubt flee with the tide to some infinitely distant shore. He would not come back to me a second time.

In my ministrations, there was a purposeless passion. Who would know? Who would know that the tears with which I washed my husband through his dying hours were shed in grief for the passing of the passion that had brightened those hours for me?

Etsuko remembered the day she hired a car and took her recumbent husband to be admitted to the hospital run by a friend, a specialist in internal medicine. Three days later the woman of the pictures came into his room and met Etsuko's wrath. How did she find out? Did she hear from one of his friends at the office? Surely they didn't know. Maybe she smelled it out as a dog would. Another woman came—three days in a row, in fact. Still another came. Sometimes the women ran into each other, glaring at each other as they went by.

Etsuko wanted no one to infringe upon their island for two. She didn't inform those in Maidemmura of Ryosuke's danger until after he had breathed his last. She still remembered the joy she felt the day her husband's illness was diagnosed. There were only three rooms on the second floor of the tiny hospital. There was a window at the end of the hall—a blank window, giving a blank view of the neighborhood.

That odor of Lysol in the hall! Estuko loved it. When her husband dropped off into short dozes, she walked up and down the hall boldly inhaling that scent, which she preferred to the outside air. The action by which this chemical purified death and disease was to her not the action of death but the action of life. This smell, for all she could tell, was the smell of life. Like the smell of morning, it stimuated her nasal passages—this relentless, cruel, chemical body odor.

Although the fever had been 104° for ten days, Etsuko still sat by the frame of her husband as it enfolded that fever, painfully seeking an outlet for it. Ryosuke was like a marathon runner at the end of the race: gasping for breath, his nostrils flaring. In his bed, his existence was the epitome of the human body involved in ever-racing track competition. Etsuko was his claque: "Just a little more! Just a little more!" Ryosuke's eyes rolled upward. His fingertips clawed for the tape, but all he grasped was the edge of his blanket, warm as hay and rank with the odor of the animal that slept in it.

The head of the hospital examined Ryosuke as he made his morning rounds and exposed his chest, alive with labored breathing. When the physician touched the fever-crammed skin, it piled up under his fingers as if about to geyser hot water. Is sickness perhaps, after all, only an acceleration of life? When the doctor applied his ivory stethoscope to Ryosuke's chest, the yellow ivory created slightly white pressure marks; then here and there in the skin suddenly charged with blood, fine, opaque, rose-colored spots floated up.

Etsuko asked about the spots: "What are they?"

"Well, now," the doctor said in a detached, yet friendly tone: "Roseola. I'll explain it to you later."

When the examination was over, he led Etsuko to the door and said drily: "It's typhoid fever. We finally got back the results of the blood tests. Where on earth did Ryosuke pick that up? He said he drank some well water while on a business trip; maybe that was it. But it's all right. If his heart can bear it, there's no problem. It's a rather strange case, though, so the diagnosis was slow in coming. Today we must take steps to move him to a hospital specializing in what he has. We don't have an isolation room here."

The doctor drummed with his dried-up knuckles on the wall posted with "No Smoking" signs, and in an attitude tinged with ennui waited for this woman with dark circles under her eyes—exhausted by days of nursing—to shout something, plead something: "Doctor! Please! Don't report it; keep him here! If you move that man, sick as he is, he'll die! Surely a man's life matters more than the law. Doctor! Don't just send him to a hospital for infectious diseases. See if you can have him placed in the isolation ward of a university hospital. Doctor!" He waited with educated curiosity for hackneyed appeals like these to issue from Etsuko's mouth.

But Etsuko said nothing.

"You're tired, aren't you?" said the doctor.

"No," said Etsuko, in a tone some might call heroic.

Etsuko was not afraid of catching typhoid. (This seemed to be the only reason she escaped it.) She returned to the chair beside her husband and went on with her knitting. Winter was coming, and she was knitting him a sweater. The room was cool in the morning. She slipped off one *zori*, then picked up that foot and rubbed the instep of the other.

"They know what I have, don't they?" asked Ryosuke, his voice lilting like a child's.

"Yes." Etsuko got up intending to sponge his dry lips, cracked in fine fissures by the fever, with a piece of wet cotton. Instead she pressed her cheek against his. His unshaven, sick man's face burned hers like hot beach sand.

"It's all right. Etsuko will make sure you get better. Don't worry about a thing. If you died, I'd die too." (Who would hold her to that false pledge? There were no witnesses anyway—not even God, whom Etsuko didn't believe in.) "But that isn't going to happen. You're going to get better; that's certain."

Etsuko kissed her husband's parched lips frenziedly. They were constantly exhaling hot breath, as if fed by subterranean heat. Etsuko's lips moistened her husband's blood-smeared lips, thorny as roses. Under his wife's face, Ryosuke's face writhed.

The gauze-wrapped door handle turned, and the door opened slightly. Etsuko heard the sound and released her husband. It was a nurse, beckoning to Etsuko with her eyes. They went out into the hall. A woman was there, in a long dress and fur cape, leaning by the window at the end of the hall.

It was the woman of the pictures. At first glance she seemed to be Eurasian. Her teeth were so lovely they looked false. Her nostrils were shaped like wings. The wet paraffin paper around the bouquet she was carrying stuck to her red fingernails. There was something impotent, frustrated, about this woman's bearing, as if she were an animal standing on its hind legs trying to walk. She could have been forty: the wrinkles in the corners of her eyes would suddenly spring out as if from ambush, belying the twenty-five years one might first have given her.

"How do you do?" the woman said. There was in her words a faint, elusive accent. Etsuko saw her as a woman stupid men might find exotic. Yet this was the woman who had caused her so much pain. Etsuko found it difficult at this short notice to bring together that past pain and this present embodiment of its cause. Her pain had already matured (strange way of saying it!) to the point at which it was something imaginative, having no connection with this concrete entity. The woman was an extracted tooth; it hurt her no more. Like a sick man who has weathered all the little, phony illnesses and now is face to face with the killer itself, Etsuko found herself demeaned by the thought that this woman had been the cause of all her troubles.

The woman held out a calling card with a man's name on it, saying she had come in her husband's place. On the card was the name of the general manager of the firm for which Ryosuke worked. "He is not supposed to have visitors," Etsuko said; "no one is allowed in." Something like a shadow darted across the woman's eyes.

"But my husband asked me to see him and find out how he is."

"Well, that's how my husband is: no one can see him."

"If I could just look in at him, my husband would be satisfied."

"If your husband were here I would let him in."

"Why is it that my husband could go in, but I can't? That doesn't make sense. The way you talk makes me feel you're worried about something."

"All right, nobody is to go in to see him. Does that satisfy you?"

"I find the way you speak extraordinary. Are you his wife—Ryosuke's wife?"

"I am the only woman who calls my husband 'Ryosuke!' "

"Please, may I, please, just look in at him? I beg of you. Here, this is not much, but I thought it would brighten up his room."

"Thank you."

"Mrs. Sugimoto, may I see him? How is he? He isn't seriously ill, is he?"

"He may live, and he may die—no one knows."

Etsuko's derisive tone shook the woman. She threw etiquette aside and said: "Well, if that's the way it is, I'm going to see him whether you like it or not."

"Come right this way. If you don't mind going in, make yourself at home." Etsuko turned and led the way back to the room. "Do you know what my husband has?"

"No."

"Typhoid."

The woman stopped, her color changing. "Typhoid?" she whispered.

Here was an uncouth woman, surely. Her shocked reaction was that of the old wife who upon hearing someone has tuberculosis says: "Heavens preserve us!" She might even go so far as to cross herself! This foreigner's concubine! What was she waiting for? Etsuko amiably opened the door. The woman's startled reaction pleased Etsuko. She moved the chair at her husband's bedside even closer to him.

The woman had no choice but to move cautiously into the room. Etsuko took boundless pleasure in having her husband see the woman's trepidation.

The woman took off her cape but didn't know what to do with it. Any place where bacteria might adhere was out of the question. Even Etsuko's hand was suspect, for she certainly emptied her husband's bedpans. It seemed wisest to keep it on. She slipped her shoulders into it again. Then she dragged the chair back several feet and sat down.

Etsuko relayed the name on the calling card to her husband. Ryosuke shot a look at the woman but said nothing. The woman crossed her legs. She sat pale and silent.

Etsuko stood as if she were a nurse behind the visitor and watched her husband's expression. A sudden anxious thought took her breath away: *What if my husband doesn't love this woman at all? What then? Then all my suffering has no basis, and my husband and I have been torturing each other in a ridiculous charade; my recent past is nothing more than a meaningless performance of shadow-boxing. Now I must find in my husband's eyes some infinitesimal sign of love for this woman, or I won't be able to go on. If he loves neither her nor the three other women whom I did not allow in to see him, how, after all that has happened, can I bear it?*

Ryosuke, still looking toward the ceiling, moved under his quilt, which was already somewhat askew. He raised his knees; the quilt began to slide to the floor. The woman shrank back somewhat. She did not so much as extend her hand. Etsuko ran to set the bed in order.

In that space of a few seconds, Ryosuke turned his face toward his visitor. Involved as she was with the quilt, Etsuko couldn't see them. Her intuition told her, however, that in those moments her husband and the woman had exchanged winks, two winks that denigrated her. This man with a fever raging had smiled and winked at this woman.

It was not really intuition. It was surmise, rather, based on a movement she perceived in her husband's cheek. She surmised it and thus experienced a sense of relief barred to those who judge by ordinary powers of understanding.

"You'll have no trouble recovering from this. It can't really hurt somebody with your nerve." The woman's tone had suddenly lost its reserve.

A gentle smile played over Ryosuke's unshaved features —had he ever turned this smile on Etsuko? Then he said, his voice lilting: "It's too bad I can't give this illness to you. You'd outlast it."

"Why, how dare you?" She laughed, looking at Etsuko for the first time.

"I can't outlast it," Ryosuke persisted. There was an awkward silence. The woman suddenly laughed a chirping laugh.

A few minutes later she left.

That night brain fever set in. The typhoid bacillus had attacked Ryosuke's brain.

The radio in the downstairs waiting room blared noisy jazz. "I can't stand it," Ryosuke moaned as his head throbbed violently. "I'm sick as a dog and that radio goes . . ."

The lightbulb in the sickroom had been covered with a *furoshiki* so that the glare did not bother the sick man's eyes. Etsuko had climbed on a chair and tied it there without even bothering to call a nurse for help. The light coming through the muslin had the unfortunate effect of imparting a greenish cast to Ryosuke's face. In this strange green umbra his bloodshot eyes seemed overwhelmed by anger and tears.

Etsuko put down her knitting and stood up. "I'm going downstairs," she said; "I'll ask them to turn it down." As she reached the door she heard behind her a bone-chilling groan.

It was a cry that might have been emitted by an animal being stepped on. Etsuko turned; Ryosuke was sitting up in bed. He clutched the quilt in both hands as a child might. His eyes stared blankly yet fixedly toward the door.

The nurse heard and came into the room. She helped stretch Ryosuke's body out, as if unfolding a collapsible chair, and placed his hands back under the covers. The sick man submitted, groaning all the while; then after a time he called, rolling his eyes from side to side: "Etsuko! Etsuko!"

Etsuko heard and wondered how, of all the names he

should be calling, he had chosen this one. He seemed not to be following his own will so much as hers. She had the strange conviction that he was saying this name at her command, as if reciting a rule.

"Say it again," she said.

The nurse had left to call the doctor. Etsuko bent over as she spoke, took her husband by the arms, and cruelly shook him. Again he gasped: "Etsuko! Etsuko!"

Late that night, Ryosuke shouted indistinctly: "It's black! It's black!" Then he propelled himself from his bed and knocked the medicine bottles and pitcher off the table, after which he walked around on the broken glass, cutting his feet horribly. Three men, including the janitor, came running and restrained him.

The next day he was injected with sedatives, placed on a stretcher, and loaded into an ambulance. He was an unusually heavy burden. It was raining. Etsuko held an umbrella over him from the door of the hospital to the gate where the ambulance waited.

The Hospital for Infectious Diseases. With great joy Etsuko welcomed that ugly building, on the other side of the steel bridge that threw its shadow on the broken pavement of the road. Life on an island, life in its ideal form, which Etsuko had always pined for, was about to begin. Nobody could follow them here. Nobody could get in. The only people who lived here were those who made resistance to germs their only reason for being. Unceasing approbation of life; a rough, rude approbation that did not care at all about appearances. An approbation of life beyond law and beyond morality, dramatized and incessantly demanded by delirium, incontinence, bloody excrement, vomit, diarrhea, and horrible odors. This air which, like a mob of merchants shouting bids at a produce auction, craved in every second the call: "Still alive! Still alive!" This busy terminal where life constantly came and went, arrived and departed, boarded and debarked. This mass of active bodies, unified by the unique form of existence they bore, namely, contagious disease. Here the value of men's lives and germs' lives frequently came to the same thing; patient and practitioner were metamorphosed into bacteria —into such objectless life. Here life existed only for the sake of being affirmed; no pettier desire was allowed. Here happiness reigned. In fact, here happiness, that most rapidly rotting of all foods, reigned in its most rotten, most inedible form.

Etsuko lived life to the full here among death and evil odors. Her husband was constantly befouled; on the day after he arrived here, he passed bloody stools. The dreaded intestinal bleeding had begun.

Although his high fever continued unabated, he lost neither weight nor color. On his hard, uninviting bed, his lustrous pink body lay like a baby's. He didn't have enough energy to toss. He lay listlessly, both hands holding his stomach or stroking his chest with fists doubled up. His fingers ineptly played under his nostrils as he inhaled that odor.

As for Etsuko, her existence was now one fixed stare. Her eyes had forgotten how to close, like unprotected open windows mercilessly searched by wind and rain. The nurses were amazed at her mad, feverish ministrations. She took only an hour or two of sleep a day at the side of this half-naked husband reeking of urine. Even then she would dream that he was being dragged away into some deep ditch calling her name, and she would wake.

The attending physician suggested blood transfusions as a last resort, hinting vaguely at the same time that he didn't expect them to do any good. As a result of the transfusions, Ryosuke became rather calm and slept continuously. A nurse came in with the bill. Etsuko went out into the hall with her.

A boy stood there, his bad skin color partly concealed by the hunting cap he wore. When he saw Etsuko, he removed his hat and silently bowed. At one small spot above his left ear he had no hair. His eyes had a slight squint; his nose was extremely thin.

"Yes, what can I do for you?" Etsuko asked. The boy did not answer but simply toyed with his cap and scraped meaningless circles on the floor boards with his right foot. "Oh, this?" said Etsuko, holding out the bill. The boy nodded.

Etsuko watched the dirty jacket of the boy as he departed with his money and thought about that boy's blood circulating inside Ryosuke. *As if that was going to save him! Couldn't they get blood from someone who had some to spare? Taking that boy's blood was a crime. A man with blood to spare?* Her thoughts moved restlessly to Ryosuke in his sickbed. *It would make more sense to sell Ryosuke's germ-laden surfeit of blood. Sell that to healthy people. Then Ryosuke would become healthy and the healthy people sick. And the city would know that it was getting its money's worth out of the Hospital for Infectious Diseases. But Ryosuke—it wouldn't do to have him become healthy. If he were well he would take off again.*

Etsuko realized that her thoughts were running on confusedly—half-dream, half-waking. It seemed as if the sun had suddenly gone down; everything around her seemed in shadow. The windows stood in a line, each filled with a stark-white, clouded evening sky. Etsuko staggered and fainted.

It was a slight attack of cerebral ischemia. The doctors insisted she take a short period of rest. After four hours, however, a nurse came in to tell her Ryosuke was dying.

Ryosuke's lips seemed to be trying to say something through the oxygen inhalator Etsuko held before him. What was it that his lips were inaudibly forming, incessantly, desperately, and yet rather joyfully?

I held the inhalator with all the power I could muster. In the end my hands cramped; my shoulders went numb. I called in what must have been close to a scream: "Somebody take over for me. Quickly!" The nurse jumped up in a flurry and took the inhalator from me.

Really, I wasn't tired or anything; I was simply frightened. Frightened of those inaudible words my husband was uttering as he lay there facing he knew not what . . . Was it my jealousy again? Or was it my fear of my jealousy? I did not know. If I had lost control of myself, I might have screamed: "Die, will you! Die!"

There was evidence that I might. Far into the night, as his heart continued to beat, showing no signs of quitting, and two of the doctors stood up and walked off to bed whispering to each other, "I wouldn't be surprised if he's going to make it," I watched them go with eyes full of hate. Was he not going to die after all? That night was the night of our last battle.

At that time, as I saw it, the uncertain happiness I divined for my husband and me if he recovered, and the present hopelessness that he would live were just about the same thing. Thus it seemed to me that now at any moment I would find happiness. But not that uncertain happiness! It was much easier to contemplate my husband's certain death rather than his uncertain life. My hopes for my husband's life, somehow maintained moment after moment, and my prayers for his death amounted to the same thing. But his body lived on! He would betray me!

"He's probably at the crisis now," the doctor had said hopefully. Jealousy swept over me. Tears fell on my right hand, which was holding Ryosuke's face. My left hand, at the same time, struggled to pull the inhalator away from his mouth. In a chair nearby the nurse slept. The room was getting colder as the night deepened. Through the window I could see the signals of the Shinjuku station coming out of the darkness, and the lights of neon signs revolving through the night. The sound of train whistles, mingling with the sounds of passing car horns, cut through the atmosphere. I had a woolen shawl over my shoulders to protect my neck from the penetrating cold.

If I pulled away the inhalator now, no one would know. There was nobody to see it. I didn't believe in any witnessing agency other than men's eyes. Yet I couldn't do it. I went on till dawn holding the inhalator alternately in each hand. What were the powers that made me hold back? Love? No, never. My love would have wanted him dead. Reason? No, not that either. Reason would have needed only the certainty that no one was watching. Cowardice? Not at all. After all I wasn't even afraid of catching typhoid fever! I still don't know what the powers were.

I found out, though, in the coldest hour before daybreak, that no untoward action was necessary. The sky was turning white. Great sections of cloud waiting to reflect the glow of morning's coming stood in the heavens, but all they could do at this early hour was lend the sky a cast of severity. Suddenly Ryosuke's breathing became extremely irregular. As a child who has had enough turns his face suddenly from the breast, so he turned his face from the inhalator—as if the cord that held him had broken. I was not surprised. I placed the inhalator beside him on the pillow and took my hand mirror from my sash. It was a keepsake from my mother—who died when I was young. It was an old-fashioned mirror, backed in red brocade. I brought it close to my husband's mouth; the glass did not cloud. His lips, fringed with whiskers and pouting, appeared in the mirror bright and clear.

* * * *

Was Etsuko's acceptance of Yakichi's invitation to come to Maidemmura perhaps based on the same resolve as that which had brought her to the Hospital for Infectious Diseases? Was coming here like returning there?

Didn't the air of the Sugimoto family seem to be, the more she inhaled it, the air of the hospital? An overpowering, corrupting spirit seemed to hold her in invisible chains.

It was in the very middle of April, that night when Yakichi came to Etsuko's room to press her to finish some mending she was doing for him.

Until ten o'clock that evening, the whole household—including Etsuko, Kensuke and his wife, Asako and her two children, as well as Saburo and Miyo—had been in the eight-mat workroom busy making bags for the loquats, a little behind schedule. In normal years the task of making bags began early in April, but this year a bumper crop of bamboo sprouts had taken up their attention and made them late. If one did not cover the loquats with a bag while they were still the diameter of a fingertip, weevils would get into them and suck out the juices. Thus, as they went about fashioning the many thousand bags required, each person had beside him a pile of pages from old magazines, to which he applied the flour-and-water paste from a basin in the middle of the group. They were competing with each other, and many were the interesting pages they had to fold without reading.

Kensuke's impatience with this night work was vociferous. His folding was punctuated by incessant griping: "How I hate this. It's real coolie labor. I don't see any reason why we have to do this. Father's gone to bed, I'll bet. That's just like him. But why do we sit here obediently working? What if we revolted? If we don't fight for a raise or something he'll keep right on with what he's been doing. How about it, Chieko? Shall we ask for double what we're getting? Of course, I get nothing, so twice that will amount to the same thing. Look at this magazine: 'The Determination of the Japanese People over the North China Revolt.' How do you like that? And on the other side: 'Wartime Menus for Four Seasons.' "

Thanks to observations of this kind, Kensuke was barely able to paste two bags in the time everyone else made ten. Sometimes it seemed that all his wild complaints were designed to hide his embarrassment at the fact that his complete lack of self-sufficiency was so abundantly clear. Chieko saw a cynical heroism in the clownish pose he assumed voluntarily lest he fall into it involuntarily. She took pride in her ability to be as quarrelsome as he, yet she extended to her husband whole-hearted adulation. She recognized that as a good wife she should share her husband's anger against her father-in-law, and along with her husband she despised Yakichi in her heart. While she folded her own share of bags, she quietly and ingeniously lent a hand to complete her husband's allotment. Etsuko's mouth unconsciously fell into a smile as she watched Chieko's unobtrusive self-abnegation.

"You're fast, Etsuko, aren't you?" said Asako.

"Half-time score!" said Kensuke, and went around counting the bags each had completed. Etsuko was first, with 380.

Etsuko's skill was lost on the insensitive Asako and on the unreflectively admiring Saburo and Miyo, but to Kensuke and his wife it was vaguely unsettling, a fact Etsuko herself perceived. To Kensuke in particular the very number she had attained was the index of her ability to survive, and at the same time it was a patent slur, on which he commented sarcastically: "Well, it looks like Etsuko's the only one of us that could live off folding bags."

Asako took him literally and asked: "Have you had experience folding envelopes, Etsuko?"

Etsuko found nothing appealing in the cloying class prejudice these people seemed to derive from their pitiful, niggling, country respectability. As one who had the blood of a famous general of the civil wars, Etsuko could not pardon their upstart pride. She struck out against it with a deliberately combative reply: "As a matter of fact, I have."

Kensuke and Chieko exchanged looks. That night the

subject of their intense bedtime conversation was the ancestry that permitted Etsuko such coolness.

At that time Etsuko paid no attention worthy of the word to Saburo's existence. Later she could not remember clearly what he looked like. That was natural enough, since Saburo said not a word, smiled only occasionally at the prattle of his employer's family, and clumsily applied his fingertips to the task of pasting up the paper bags. Over his usual patched shirt, he wore one of Yakichi's old, overly-roomy suit coats, and sat respectfully in his brand-new khaki-colored trousers, head bent down in the dim light.

Up until eight or nine years earlier, the Sugimoto family had used Blanchard lamps. Those who remembered back that far said the rooms had been brighter then. Since the electricity had been installed, unfortunately, they had to light hundred-watt bulbs with a piddling forty watts of power. The radio was audible only at night and, under certain weather conditions, not even then.

Yet it wasn't true that she did not pay any attention to him. As she folded her bags, Etsuko at times noticed how clumsy Saburo's fingers were. Those stubby, ruggedly honest fingertips irritated her. She looked to the side and saw Chieko helping her husband fold his quota. The vague notion came to her that she might do the same for Saburo. She perceived, however, that Miyo, sitting over beside Saburo, quietly helped him when her assigned lot was complete. This relieved her.

I felt relieved then. Yes, without the slightest jealousy or anything like it. In fact I felt a faint joy at being divested of responsibility. I tried not to watch what Saburo was doing.

That was easy enough. My bent back, my silence, my application to the task—all without seeing him—aped Saburo's silence, Saburo's bent posture, Saburo's application to the task.

. . . yet there wasn't a thing.

Eleven o'clock came. Everyone withdrew to their rooms.

What did she feel, then, when at one in the morning Yakichi, smoking his pipe, came into her room while she was mending and asked how she had been sleeping lately? This old man with ears turned toward Etsuko's bedroom every night—ears alive all night to the turnings and wakings of Etsuko in the room down the hall. Are not old men's ears like pure shells, incessantly washed and filled with wisdom? The ears, which in shape seem more like the property of an animal than any other part of the human body, are in an old man the very incarnation of intelligence. Was it for these reasons that Etsuko saw something other than ugliness in Yakichi's solicitude on her behalf? Was it as if she were guarded and loved by wisdom?

And yet giving it such a lovely name is perhaps going too far. Yakichi stood behind Etsuko, looking at her calendar on a doorpost.

"What's this? You bad girl. It's still at last week's date," he said.

Etsuko turned slightly: "Is it? I beg your pardon."

"Beg pardon? You don't have to say that."

His voice was filled with good humor; as he spoke Etsuko could hear behind her the sound of pages being torn from her calendar. Then all sound stopped. She suddenly felt her shoulder being grasped, while a cold hand dry as bamboo slipped into her bodice. Her body recoiled slightly, but she said nothing. It was not because she could not cry out; she simply didn't.

How can one explain the sense of resignation Etsuko felt at this moment? Was it simply lust? Sloth? Was it the way a thirst-crazed man swallows rusty water that Etsuko accepted this? No. Etsuko was not thirsty in the slightest. Her nature had suddenly become one that asked for nothing. It seemed as if she had come to Maidemmura to find again a basis for that fearful self-sufficiency she had contracted in the Hospital for Infectious Diseases. She drank perhaps like a drowning man helplessly swallowing sea water, in accordance with some law of nature. Not to ask for anything means that one has lost one's freedom to choose or reject. Once having decided that, one has no choice but to drink anything—even sea water . . .

Afterward, however, Etsuko exhibited none of the gagging expressions of a drowning person. Until the moment of her death, it seemed, no one would know she was drowning. She did not call out—this woman bound and gagged by her own hand . . .

April eighteenth was the day for the "mountain journey," as they called cherry-blossom viewing in this area. It was the custom for everyone to take the day off and gather in family groups to wander about the foothills looking at blossoms.

Everyone in the Sugimoto household except Yakichi and Etsuko had been eating more than they wished of *jami*—bamboo-shoot scraps. The former tenant farmer, Okura, would take the bamboo shoots they had harvested out of the shed, load them into the bicycle trailer, and take them to market, where they were graded and sold at three different prices. The bamboo shoots left over were swept up into a great pile and then cooked by the potful to make up the bill of fare for the Sugimotos other than Yakichi and Etsuko in April and May.

The day of the mountain journey, however, was a grand occasion. A whole feast had been crammed into nested boxes. Clutching decorated mats, the family started out *en masse* to enjoy their picnic. Asako's older child, a girl, was in raptures; there was no school.

Etsuko recalled: *We passed a lovely spring day, quite like those one sees boldly pictured in schoolbooks. Everyone became a person boldly painted in a picture—or played that part.*

There in the atmosphere charged with the intimate smell of manure—in the intimacy of country people, somehow the smell of manure is always present . . . And all those insects flying! And the air filled with the droning flight of bees and beetles! And the shining wind replete with sunlight! And the bellies of swallows turning in the wind!

On the morning of the mountain journey those in the house were busy with preparations. When Etsuko finished packing the *sushi* lunches, she looked through the lattice window at Asako's daughter, who was playing on the flagstone floor of the entranceway. She was dressed, in accordance with her mother's terrible taste, in a bright yellow sweater the color of mustard flowers. What was she doing—this squatting girl of eight, eyes fixed on the ground? There on the flagstones was an iron teakettle, steam rising from it. Nobuko was staring intently at something moving between the edge of the stone floor and the dirt in which it was laid.

It was a swarm of ants, floating about in the hot water

that had been poured into their nest. Countless ants writhing in the boiling water that welled from the aperture of the nest. And that eight-year-old child, her bobbed head thrust deep between her knees, was watching them silently and intently. She held both hands against her face, oblivious to the hair that slanted down over her cheeks.

As she watched this, Etsuko felt refreshed. Until the mother noticed that the kettle was gone and called to her daughter through the kitchen door, Etsuko watched Nobuko's small back with its taut yellow sweater as if it were her own at some earlier time. From this time on she felt something slightly like a mother's love toward this child ugly with her mother's features.

Just before they left, there was a little flurry as to who would stay at home. In the end, however, Miyo bowed to Etsuko's sensible suggestion that she remain. Etsuko was amazed that her rather offhand expression of opinion on the subject was followed. There was, however, nothing very complicated about it. Yakichi simply did what she wished.

As the family fell into single file on the path that led from their property to the village nearby, Etsuko was again rudely shaken by awareness that the family seemed to be unconsciously guided by an annoyingly sharp sense of social stratification. It was an acute, animal instinct, like that by which one worker ant knows simply by feel or smell another worker ant from a different nest, or the queen ant knows a worker ant, or, in turn, the worker knows the queen. They couldn't have found out . . . There was as yet no evidence by which they might . . . In the line the household group formed, however, all unwittingly, Yakichi came first, then Etsuko, then Kensuke, Chieko, Asako,

Nobuko (her younger brother Natsuo, age five, had been left with Miyo) in order down to Saburo, carrying on his shoulder a great arabesque-pattern *furoshiki* filled with provisions.

They crossed an outlying section in the back of their property; it was the area now largely fallen into disuse in which Yakichi had cultivated grapes before the war. It was a patch about one fourth of an acre in size, of which about a third was taken up by small peach trees in full bloom. The rest of it was occupied by three toppling greenhouses, their glass almost all destroyed by typhoons, oil drums filled with stagnant rainwater, grapevines returned to the wild . . . sunbeams falling on dry straw.

"This is terrible, isn't it," said Yakichi, pushing one of the posts holding up a greenhouse with his thick rattan stick. "The next time we get some money we'll fix it up."

"You're always saying that, Father," said Kensuke, "but these greenhouses will probably be like this forever."

"We never get any money; is that what you mean?"

"Not at all," said Kensuke, his voice picking up tone. "When you get any money, Father, it's always too much or too little to use for repairs."

"Now, is that so? You mean it's either too much or too little to give you as part of your allowance."

As they talked, they arrived at the top of a hill covered by pines in which four or five mountain cherries were mingled. There were no cherry trees of the famous blossoming varieties hereabout, so they had no choice but to spread their decorated mats under the mountain cherries, unsuitable for any proper blossom viewing. Already farm families had taken up the area under each of the trees. They bowed cordially as the line of the Sugimoto family arrived. They did not, however, offer their places, as they were once wont to do.

Kensuke and Chieko began whispering to each other about the other families. In accordance with Yakichi's instructions, everyone spread their mats on a portion of the slope from which they could see the blossoms in something like a panorama. A farmer of their acquaintance—a man in his fifties wearing a pink necktie under a government-issue, checkered jacket—came over carrying a bottle and *saké* cup and offered them some holiday raw *saké*. Kensuke accepted a cup and blithely drained it.

Now, why? thought Etsuko, rather disconnectedly, as she watched Kensuke. *I wouldn't have any. . . .* Her thoughts were worth little: *Now, there's Kensuke accepting the* saké *cup—he with the cutting remarks still in his mouth. It would be all right if he really liked raw* saké. *But anyone can tell he has never cared for it. He's doing it simply because he enjoys drinking* saké *given him by this man who is unaware that he has been ripped up the back. That small joy in rottenness. Joy in spite. Joy in the little laugh up one's sleeve. . . . There are some people who are born for no other purpose. God seems to enjoy doing silly things like that.*

Then Chieko took the cup—only because her husband had.

Etsuko refused. This gave all of them another reason to talk about her as a woman who did not conform.

A certain order seemed to be forming within the family circle on this day, an occurrence Etsuko found no reason to resent. She was satisfied in the relationship between the two expressionless solidities made up of Yakichi's expressionless good humor and, at his side, her own expressionless self. Next she was satisfied with Saburo—bored, with no one to talk to, not even a boy as silent as himself. She was satisfied with the dull motherliness of Asako, and even the hostility of Kensuke and his wife, hidden under the mantle of tolerance. It was an order created by Etsuko and no one else.

Nobuko bent over Etsuko, holding a small wildflower. "What is it, Aunt Etsuko?" she asked. Etsuko didn't know and asked Saburo.

Saburo glanced at the flower and returned it to Etsuko. "It's a *murasuzume*," he said.

What surprised Etsuko was not the strange name of the flower, but the blinding speed of his hand as he returned it.

Chieko, quick of hearing, caught the exchange and said: "This fellow acts as though he knows nothing, and he knows everything. Sing us a Tenri song. You'll be amazed how much he knows."

Saburo looked down, his face red.

"Please, sing. Don't be embarrassed. Sing," said Chieko, handing him a hardboiled egg. "See, I'll give you this. Sing for us."

Saburo glanced at the egg between Chieko's fingers, on one of which a ring with a cheap stone glittered. In his black puppy's eye a tiny sharp gleam moved. He said: "Forget the egg. I'll sing." Then he smiled a little smile, seemingly of apology.

Chieko said: " 'If the whole world in one line'—and something else."

" 'Lay before your eyes,' it goes," he said, his face serious. Then he turned his eyes toward the nearby village spread out before them and recited, as if repeating an imperial mandate. The village was in a small valley. In the war an army air force unit was billeted there. From its secluded recess officers commuted to Hotarugaike Air Base. Cherries grew along the creek over there. And an elementary school had a tiny yard with cherry trees in it, too. Two or three children were visible there, playing on an exercise bar built over sand. They looked like balls of lint blown in the wind.

Saburo recited this text from Tenri litany:

> I look upon the whole world stretched out in one line,
> And not a soul among them there knows what's going on.
> Of course, there is nobody to teach them.
> Nobody knows anything, which is as it should be.
> But God is appearing now before all eyes,
> And teaching everybody there every single thing.

"That was banned during the war," Yakichi commented learnedly. "Those lines 'I look upon the whole world stretched out in one line/ And not a soul among them there knows what's going on' sounded as though they included His Majesty. Logically, anyway. So the Intelligence Office banned it, I understand."

Nothing happened on that day—the day of that mountain journey—either.

A week after that Saburo was given three days off, as he was every year, so that he could go to Tenri to march in the great April Twenty-sixth Festival. He would meet his mother at the National Church, stay over there, and worship at the Mother Temple.

Etsuko had not yet been in Tenri. There was a magnificent temple there, built by the gifts of the faithful from all over the country and erected with their "*Hinoki* faith" contributions, as they referred to their donated labor. In the very center of the temple was a "manna table." She had heard stories of that table—on which on the last day manna would fall—and how, in the winter, through the roof, open like a skylight, snowflakes would come and dance in the wind.

"*Hinoki* faith"—there was in the term the smell of new wood and the sound of clear devotion and joyful labor. It told of old men who could no longer work and, just to be part of it, would scoop dirt into their handkerchiefs and help in construction.

Well, enough of that . . . In those three short days of Saburo's absence, the feeling that developed with his absence—whatever the feeling—was to me entirely new. As a gardener who, after long care and toil, holds in his hand a marvelous peach, hefts the weight of it, and feels the joy of it, so I felt the weight of his absence in my hand and reveled in it. It would not be true to say that those three days were lonely. To me his absence was a plump, fresh weight. That was joy! Everywhere in the house I perceived his absence—in the yard, in the workroom, in the kitchen, in his bedroom.

Out of the bay window of his room, his quilts were hung to air. They were thin, rough, cotton quilts with dark blue stripes. Etsuko was on her way into the back field to pick some Chinese cabbage for the evening meal. Saburo's room faced the southwest and received the sun in the afternoon. The sun lit up every corner of it, all the way to the torn partition far from the window.

Etsuko had not come here to peer into his room. She had

been drawn by the delicate fragrance floating in the western sun, the smell released by a young animal sprawled asleep in the sunlight. She stood a moment by the quilts, for just a moment by this frayed fabric with the smell and luster of leather. She pressed her finger against it out of curiosity, as if stroking something alive. A warm elasticity in the cotton, swelled in the sun, answered her touch. Etsuko departed and slowly descended the stone steps that ran under the oaks toward the back fields.

And so Etsuko finally fell again into the slumber that had long eluded her.

3

THE *SWALLOW'S NEST* was empty—since yesterday, it seemed.

The second-floor room of Kensuke and his wife had windows on the south and east. In the summer, they enjoyed watching, out their east window, the swallows that nested under the eaves of the first-floor entranceway.

Etsuko was returning a book she had borrowed from Kensuke and, as she stood leaning against the rail at the window of his room, said: "The swallows are gone, aren't they?"

"Yes, but while you're there, notice that we can see Osaka Castle today. It's so smoggy in the summer you can't see it."

Kensuke was sprawled out reading a book, which he laid aside. Then he threw open the southern window and pointed to the horizon in the southwest.

When one looked at the castle from here one could not see any part of it anchored firmly to the ground. Everything floated. Everything was suspended. When the air cleared, one could fancy seeing something like the spirit of the castle detach itself from the material castle and stretch on tiptoe and look about from that height. In Etsuko's eyes, the tower of Osaka Castle was like a spectral island constantly beguiling the gaze of a castaway.

No one lives there, I suppose, she thought. *Perhaps, somewhere, there are men living in castle towers buried in dust.*

The conclusion that no one lived there relieved her. How unhappy—an imagination that couldn't keep itself from making wild surmises as to whether someone was or was not living in some far-off old castle! It was this imagination that constantly shook the foundation of her happiness—which was to think about nothing at all.

"What are you thinking about, Etsuko? Ryosuke? Or . . ." said Kensuke, sitting in the window bay. His voice—though it was not the same at all—was somehow like Ryosuke's in its shading, and it shocked Etsuko into an honest reply.

"I was wondering if anyone lives in the castle."

Her smoky, suppressed laugh awoke Kensuke's cynicism. "You like people, after all, don't you, Etsuko? People, people, people—you are really normal—with a normality I can't even come close to. You just need to be a little honest with yourself. That's my diagnosis. If so . . ."

Chieko, who had gone down to the sink to wash the cups and plates from their late breakfast, came up the stairs carrying the dishes in a tray covered by a towel. A little package dangled perilously from her middle finger, and before she put the tray down she dropped the package in Kensuke's lap where he sat in the window.

"It came!"

"Oh! The medicine I've been waiting for?"

He opened the package and took out a little can marked "Himrod's Powder." It was an American asthma remedy that a friend of his in a trading firm in Osaka had managed to have sent over. It had seemed as if the desired medicine would never arrive, and only yesterday Kensuke had complained about his friend.

Etsuko took the opportunity to leave, but Chieko stopped her, saying: "I come back, you go. It's enough to make you wonder."

Yes, and if I stay here, I don't have to wonder what's going to come up, thought Etsuko. Kensuke and his wife had, like all bored people, a sense of kindness that was close to disease. Gossip and a pushy kindness—these two qualities peculiar to country people—had already infected Kensuke and Chieko, without their knowledge, and made them don an upper-class camouflage—a camouflage of criticism and advice.

"Don't be nasty, Chieko," said Kensuke. "I was just giving her advice. She was getting away while she could."

"Let her make her own excuses. I have some advice for Etsuko. I'd like to show her I'm on her side. Maybe I should call it goading. It's close to that."

"Go ahead, let her have it. Give it to her good."

This newlywed repartee would have been hard for any third party to endure. It was a newlywed situation comedy played every afternoon and every night to a vacant house by this bored pair set down here in the middle of the country. In fact, they never tired of their well-studied parts, their hit show, nor questioned their credentials for the roles. They would be playing them till they were eighty—under the name of Mr. and Mrs. Turtle Dove, perhaps. Etsuko resolutely turned her back on them and went down the stairs.

"Must you go?"

"Yes, I have to take Maggie for a walk. When I get back, I'll see you again."

"You have a will of iron," Chieko said.

It was a morning in the off-season on the farm, as quiet as such times in the lull of harvests are wont to be. Yakichi was in the pear orchard, looking for something to do. Atsuko, with Natsuo on her back or toddling beside her, had gone to the village distribution center to get government-issue baby food. She was accompanied by Nobuko, who had the day off for Autumnal Equinox day. Miyo was peacefully moving from room to room, cleaning. Etsuko went to the tree by the kitchen door and untied Maggie's chain.

Should she go out on the Mino road and make a long circuit as far as the neighboring village? Yakichi said that back in 1935, perhaps, when he had taken that road at night, a fox had followed him all the way to the highway. But that route took two hours. To the cemetery? That was too close.

The dog's activity at the end of the chain communicated itself to Etsuko's palm. She let Maggie go where she wished. They went into the chestnut grove, where the autumn cicadas were in voice. Sunlight spattered the ground. The *shibataké* mushrooms were already visible here and there under fallen leaves. Only Etsuko and Yakichi were permitted to eat them. Yakichi had slapped Nobuko for picking some to play with.

Every day of the slack period was another day of forced rest, all of which massed like a weight on Etsuko's spirits, like so many hours of recuperation forced on a sick man who doesn't feel ill. Sleeplessness piled up. What was there to live for in a time like this? Just living in the present made every day interminably monotonous. If she dwelt on the past, the pain of it dislocated everything. Over the landscape, over the season, the glare of the hiatus floated. Etsuko could not look at a vacation with any attitude other than that of the graduate who doesn't have them anymore.

Not even that. Even in her school days she had hated summer vacations. They were simply a duty—a duty to walk by herself, to open the door for herself, and to run out into the sunshine by herself. As a pupil she had never put on her own socks, never put on her own clothes, so that being forced every day to go out to school was the most delightful, euphoric freedom. Is there anything so mercilessly efficient at making one a slave to the languor of urbanity as a slack period on the farm?

Something was pulling at Etsuko. It was a thirst that ate at her as if it were duty—a thirst like that of the drunk who, fearing that if he takes another swig he will become sick, lifts the bottle again.

The elements of all these emotions were even in the breeze that blew through the chestnut grove. The wind had lost all the turbulence of the typhoon, and as it came, holding its breath, making the lower leaves tremble, it had the demeanor of a seducer. From the direction of the tenant farmer's house came the sound of an ax cutting wood. The charcoal-firing would begin in a month or two. On the edge of the grove, a small charcoal oven was buried, where Okura every year fired the Sugimotos' fuel.

Maggie pulled Etsuko here and there in the grove. Etsuko's languid, pregnant-woman's walk was forced to become lively. As usual, she was wearing a kimono. So that she wouldn't tear it on tree stumps, she had pulled up her skirt somewhat.

The dog followed scents busily. One could see her ribs move rapidly as she breathed.

The ground of the grove was pushed up slightly in one place. Thinking it the track of a mole, Etsuko looked down at it as the dog did. Then Etsuko picked up a faint odor of perspiration. There stood Saburo. The dog jumped upon him and licked his face.

Saburo held his mattock on his shoulder with one hand and, laughing, attempted to beat the dog down with the other. The dog insisted on leaping about, however, and he had to say: "Ma'am, pull back on the chain, please!"

Etsuko came to her senses and pulled the chain.

During these past few moments of absentmindedness, what she had been watching was the mattock on his shoulder leaping repeatedly in the air as his body writhed powerfully to keep the dog down. It was a bouncing, dancing motion—the blue blade, half covered with mud, catching the sun as it came through the trees. *Watch out! What if that blade came down upon me?*

In that clear consciousness of peril, she felt strangely relaxed; she stood unmoving.

"Where are you working?" she asked. Since she was standing still, Saburo did not walk on. If they talked here and turned back, Chieko would see them walking together from her second-floor window. If she went on, Saburo would have to turn back. These quick calculations led Etsuko to remain where she was as they spoke.

"In the eggplant patch. I thought I'd turn over the places where we took plants out."

"Can't you do that in the spring?"

"Yes, but things are quiet now."

"You can't sit still, can you?"

"That's right."

Etsuko looked long at Saburo's slim, tanned neck. She found appealing this inner abundance that made it impossible for him to keep from taking up his hoe. Then she was struck by the fact that this insensitive young man, much as she did, found the agricultural off-season a bother.

Then she glanced at his torn sneakers, pulled over bare feet.

If the people who say awful things about me knew how long I've hesitated about giving him socks, I wonder what they'd think. The people of the village think I'm a fallen woman. Just the same they do with perfect composure things that are much worse than I would do. Why can't I act? I ask nothing. I wish that some morning, while my eyes are closed, the whole world would change. It's about time it came—that morning, pure morning. It would belong to no one, in answer to nobody's prayer, that morning. I dream of a moment when, without my asking, my actions will betray completely this part of me that asks for nothing. Tiny, imperceptible actions . . .

Yes, last night I felt that just thinking about giving Saburo two pairs of socks would be comfort enough. Now I'm not so sure. If I give him the socks, what will happen? He'll smile a little, hem and haw a little, and then say, "Thank you." Then he'll turn his back and go away. I can see it now—I'll be only too sad.

Who could know how many months of troubled thought I have passed contemplating this painful alternative. From the Tenri Spring Festival late in April—May, June, the long spring rains; July, August, a cruel summer; then September. Somehow I would like to know again the terrible, fearful affirmation I knew when my husband died. That would be happiness surely.

Etsuko's thoughts took another tack. *Yet, I'm happy. Nobody has the right to say that at this moment I'm anything but happy!*

She slowly and dramatically took from her sleeve the two pairs of socks.

"Look, a present! I bought them for you yesterday in the Hankyu."

Saburo returned Etsuko's look squarely, and—as Etsuko saw it—questioningly. Yet there was in his glance nothing but the most innocent of queries. There was not the slightest suspicion. He simply didn't understand why this ever-distant matron older than he should out of a clear sky give him some socks. Then it struck him that it would be impolite of him to stand here too long saying nothing. He smiled and, after wiping his muddy hands on the back of his trousers, accepted the socks and said: "Thank you very much." Then he brought the heels of his sneakers together smartly and saluted. When he saluted he always struck his heels together.

"It won't do to tell anyone you got them from me," said Etsuko.

"As you wish," he said. Then he pushed the new socks unceremoniously into his pocket and left.

That was all there was; nothing happened.

Was this all there was to be of the thing that Etsuko had waited and hoped for since the evening before? Of course not. To her this small occurrence was as carefully planned as a ceremony—minutely projected. Beginning with this small occurrence, a transfiguration would take place within her. Clouds would drift in; the face of the fields would darken; the landscape would become something of different import. Over human life, too, for a moment this change would seem to come and abide. It was just a tiny alteration in one's way of looking at things, this change by which life would come to seem completely different.

Etsuko was arrogant enough to believe that this change could come about all by itself—this change that would not be accomplished unless the eyes of human beings were changed to the eyes of wild boars. She still would not admit it: that we, as long as we have the eyes of men, no matter how our way of looking at things might change, will all in the end come up with the same answer.

The rest of that day was suddenly very busy. It was a strange day.

Etsuko emerged from the chestnut grove onto the bank of the creek, deep in vegetation. At her side was the wooden bridge that led into the Sugimoto property. On the other side of the creek was the bamboo forest. This creek would meet with the brook that ran along the Garden of Souls, merge with that, and suddenly change direction to flow northeastward, where the ricefields lay.

Maggie looked down at the stream and started barking at some children wading in the water fishing for carp. The children jeered at the old setter and shouted rude approximations of what they had heard their parents say about the young widow they could not see but assumed was at the other end of the dog's chain. When Etsuko appeared on the bank of the creek, the children climbed the far bank, waving their fishing baskets wildly, and fled into the sunlit bamboo thicket. The lower leaves of the bamboos deep in the bright grove waved meaningfully, as if the children were hiding there.

Then a bicycle bell sounded from within the thicket. Soon the mailman appeared on the bridge, walking beside his bicycle. This mailman, of forty-five or -six, had made himself unpopular with his habit of asking people to give him things.

Etsuko went to the bridge and took the telegram he held. "If you don't have a name stamp, sign please," said the mailman. (He said: "*Sainu*"—English usage that had already penetrated this far into the country.) He stared at the little ball-point pen Etsuko took out.

"What kind of pen is that?"

"A ball-point pen. They're not very expensive."

"It's odd, isn't it? May I look at it?"

Etsuko made him a gift of it—ungrudgingly, for it seemed he would admire it forever. Then she climbed the steps with Yakichi's telegram in her hand. She was amused. All the difficulty she had had in giving Saburo just two pairs of socks; and yet how easily she had given that nuisance of a mailman a ball-point pen! *That's the way it should be. If it weren't for love, people would get along fine. If it weren't for love . . .*

The Sugimoto family had sold their telephone, along with their Bechstein piano. The telegraph now served for the phone; even matters of little urgency were communicated to them by telegraph from Osaka. The family did not find telegrams unusual, even in the middle of the night.

When Yakichi opened this telegram, however, his face filled with joy. It had been sent by Keisaku Miyahara, the minister of state. He had been Yakichi's immediate successor as president of Kansai Shipping Corporation, and after the war had ventured into politics. He was now on his way to Kyushu to make a round of election speeches. He had a half-day's time and wished to stop by to see Yakichi for thirty or forty minutes. The most surprising thing was that the day of the visit was today.

Yakichi was entertaining a guest at that moment, an executive of the local farm bureau. Though the heat of the midday sun was still fierce, this man walked around collecting assessments with his jacket draped over his shoulders like a bathrobe. The Young Men's League had complained that corruption was rife among executive board members, and so this summer a new election had been held. This man, who had been newly elected to the board, made it his business to go around humbly asking the opinions of the old property owners. This area was a stronghold of the Conservative party, and he believed that practices such as this were the latest fashion.

He saw that Yakichi's face had lighted up when he read the telegram, so he asked what good news the wire had brought. Yakichi hesitated, as if in possession of a happy secret he did not wish immediately to divulge. He could not, however, keep it to himself. Too much self-control is bad for old bodies.

"It's a wire from Minister of State Miyahara, who says

he's coming by to spend a few relaxed minutes. Since it's an informal visit, I would appreciate your not telling the people of the village. Since he's doing this for his physical welfare, it wouldn't be right of me to let him be bothered. Young Miyahara was in school a class or so behind me, and joined Kansai Shipping two years after I did."

The two sofas and eleven chairs in the drawing room, long untouched by human hand, were very much like girls worn out with waiting. Above their white linen slipcovers floated an aura of desiccation beyond remedy. Yet, standing in this room, Etsuko's heart somehow felt rested. On sunny days, it was her duty to open the windows of this room at nine o'clock in the morning. When she did so the eastern windows let in the rays of the morning sun. In this season, those rays barely reached the cheeks of Yakichi's bronze bust.

One morning not long after Etsuko's arrival at Maidemmura, she was surprised to see a number of butterflies—evidently resting within a bunch of mustard flowers in a vase, waiting until this very moment—rise as the window was opened and crowd, with wings flapping, into the outside air.

With Miyo's help Etsuko tidied the room with feather dusters and dustcloths. They even dusted the glass case that enclosed the stuffed bird of paradise. They could not, however, wipe away the smell of mildew imbedded in furniture and woodwork.

"I wish we could do something about this moldy smell," Etsuko said as she polished the bronze bust and looked about her. Miyo did not answer. The seemingly half-asleep country girl was standing in a chair listlessly dusting the framed calligraphy.

"The smell is awful," said Etsuko again, as if she were, however clearly, talking to herself.

Miyo looked over from her stance in the chair and said: "Yes, it's awful—really."

Etsuko was angry. As her anger grew, she reflected on the dull rustic stolidity that characterized both Saburo and Miyo. To the extent that Saburo's comforted her Miyo's made her angry. There was only one reason: Miyo and Saburo were much more like each other than she and Saburo. That was what made her angry.

Etsuko tried sitting down in the chair Yakichi would cordially offer to the minister this evening. As she did so her face took on the magnanimity tinged with compassion appropriate to a busy man surveying the living room of a friend forgotten by the world. The minister would be taking, it seemed, several minutes of his day, of which each minute and each second were practically objects at auction, and would be ceremonially carrying them and proffering them to his host as the only gifts of this visit.

"Things are fine as they are. It's not necessary to prepare," Yakichi had said to Etsuko, with a happy look on his sour face. This great officer's visit could even bring about an unexpected renaissance in Yakichi: "How about it? Why don't you come out again and stand for office? The time when new postwar men who didn't know a thing ran rampant is gone; the time is coming back in government and business for their great forerunners, rich with experience."

Yakichi would hear this, and his ridicule, wearing the mask of self-deprecation, would quickly take wing and shine as only it could shine.

"I'm through. This silly old man here is not good for a thing. Maybe I can imitate a farmer; but 'Old men shouldn't take cold showers,' as they say. All I'm good for, really, is fiddling with *bonsai*, or something like that. But I don't have any regrets. I'm satisfied as I am. I don't know whether I should say this to your face, but in this time, I believe, nothing is more perilous than standing in the forefront of the age. No one knows when it's going to turn upside down, does one? It's a rigged world. Peace is rigged. By the same token, war is rigged and the prosperity is rigged. And in this rigged world a lot of people live and die.

"Of course, all men live and die. It's a matter of course. But in this rigged world, you don't find anything to lay down your life for. Don't you see? In a *rigged life* it has become stupid to *risk* one's *life*. Yet a fellow like me can't work without laying his life on the line. No, I'm not the only one. In fact, as I see it, nobody can do his work right without risking his life. But all there are around today are sad characters who carry on even though they don't have jobs they would lay down their lives for. That's how it seems, anyway. That's how bad it is. And that's why I'm an old man, with not much more to go.

"But don't get upset. Just take it as so much whistling in the dark. I'm an old fogy—just so much dregs. Only fit to be ground up for soup. To press these dregs again into second-rate *saké* would be a sad story indeed."

The blandishments Yakichi would waft before the senses

of the minister might have been packaged under the name "Rest and Seclusion," so seductively would they draw him away from fame and fortune. What would they profit Yakichi? They would give social value to his seclusion, foster overestimation of the sharpness of the talons this world-sick old hawk held concealed.

> Mornings, drink the dew from the magnolias;
> Evenings, eat the petals dropped from the chrysanthemums.

It was Yakichi's favorite quotation from the Chinese classic the *Li Sao*, written in his own calligraphy and hung in a frame on the wall of the reception room. To a parvenu, developing a hobby like this is a considerable achievement. Since only one personal eccentricity was enough to mature his taste for hobbies, this tenant-farmer penchant for calligraphy had evidently put a brake on Yakichi's ambitions. People who are well born, however, seldom steep themselves thus in elegance.

Until well into the afternoon the household was very busy. Yakichi said over and over that an extravagant reception was not necessary. All understood, however, that if they took him at his word he would be very upset. Only Kensuke quietly skulked on the second floor, avoiding the work. Etsuko and Chieko deftly arranged the Autumnal Equinox rice cakes in matching lacquered boxes. They made whatever preparations they could in the event their guests stayed for the evening meal, going so far as to include portions for a secretary and a chauffeur. Mrs. Okura was called to strangle the chicken. When she started for the chicken coop in her house dress, Asako's children both ran along, curious as to what was happening.

"Now, don't be naughty! Haven't I always told you that you shouldn't watch chickens being strangled?" their mother called from the house. Asako couldn't cook or sew, yet she thought herself liberally endowed with the faculty of bringing up children in the *petit-bourgeois* tradition. She had flown into a passion, for instance, when Nobuko came in with a cheap comic book borrowed from the Okuras' daughter. She took it away and substituted for it a picture book for learning English. Nobuko smeared the Queen's face with blue pastel paints to get back at her mother.

As she took from the cupboard the Shunkei lacquered trays and wiped them one by one, Etsuko quivered in expectation of the screams of the chicken being strangled. She would cloud a spot with her breath, then wipe. The amber lacquer would cloud over and then clear and reflect her face. Amid these uneasy repetitions, Etsuko sketched in her mind the scene at the shed in which the chicken was being killed.

The shed gave off the kitchen door. Dangling a chicken, the bandy-legged Mrs. Okura entered. The interior was half lighted by the rays of the afternoon sun. As a result, the darker areas seemed even darker. Dull, dim outlines reflected from wrought-iron surfaces suggested the presence of mattocks and spades propped in back. Two or three weathered storm shutters leaned against the wall. There was a straw basket for carrying earth. There was a sprayer for fogging magnesium sulfate over the persimmon trees. The wife sat down in a small lopsided chair and scissored the wings of the struggling bird tightly between her thick, gnarled knees. Then, for the first time, she noticed the two children standing in the door of the shed watching her every movement, her every exertion.

"Naughty! Young lady, you're going to catch it from your mother. Now go right away from there. This isn't something children should be watching."

The chicken squawked; the chickens in the henhouse heard and squawked too.

Nobuko and little Natsuo, holding his sister's hand, with only their eyes gleaming in the shadow thrown by the light at their backs, stood and watched barely breathing as Mrs. Okura bent over the struggling chicken, writhing its whole body in the effort to free its wings. She perfunctorily reached forth both her hands toward the neck . . .

After a time Etsuko heard the chicken's screech—tentative, yet committed; full of frustration, bewilderment, and terror.

It was just four o'clock. Yakichi had managed to hide his exasperation that his guest had not yet arrived; he had even managed to act as if he were not quite worn out with waiting. As the shadows darkened under the *kaede* trees in the garden, however, he began to assume an undisguised expression of uneasiness. He went into a wild fit of smoking and then suddenly headed out to work in the pear orchard.

Etsuko attempted to help him by going out to where the highway ended at the cemetery gate to watch for a limousine destined for the Sugimoto home. She leaned against the girders of the bridge and looked far out on the distant gentle curve of the road. As she looked from this point beyond which the highway was unpaved and in fact unfinished, and watched the road twist as far as the eye could see—among rich ricefields almost ready for harvesting, cornfields with their straight rows, forests grounded in tiny swamps, the Hankyu electric line, village streets, creeks—Etsuko felt herself grow dizzy. To imagine that a limousine was going to negotiate this road to Etsuko's feet went beyond dreaming; it seemed to verge on the miraculous. According to the children, two or three cars had stopped here about noon. Now, however, there was no sign of them.

Of course, today is the Equinox! But what have we been doing? All the bean-jam rice cakes we've been making since morning, and packing them away in nested boxes in the cupboard so the children wouldn't find them and ruin them! We were so busy that not one of us thought of it. I did pray once in front of the ancestral tablets. But otherwise we only burned incense, as we do every day. All day we spent our time grieving about the arrival of living guests, and all of us forgot completely about the dead.

She watched a family troop noisily out of the gate of the Hattori Garden of Souls—an ordinary middle-aged couple and four children, one of them a girl in student dress. The children had trouble staying with the group; they constantly lagged, then ran ahead. Etsuko noticed they were playing a game, catching grasshoppers in the grass circle enclosed by the drive in which cars turned around. The winner was the one who caught the most grasshoppers without stepping on the grass. The lawn slowly darkened. The graves that lay far beyond the entrance and the thick stands of bushes and trees gradually filled with darkness, like cotton soaking up water. Only the cemetery area on the farthest slope was bright with the setting sun; the gravestones and the evergreen shrubs there shone red. The slope seemed like a face lighted by quiet rays.

Etsuko looked scornfully at the middle-aged parents, walking along talking and smiling, oblivious to the children. In her romantic way of looking at things, husbands were always unfaithful, wives always suffered; middle-aged couples all ended up not speaking to each other for one of two reasons: either they were sick of one another or hated each other. This gentleman in stylish striped sport coat and slacks, however, and his wife in her lavender suit carrying a shopping bag out of which a thermos bottle protruded seemed to be utter strangers to the romantic tale. They seemed to belong to that class that turns the romances of our world into topics for afterdinner conversation and forgets about them.

When they got as far as the bridge, the couple called their children. As they did so, they looked uneasily up and down the road otherwise devoid of humanity. Finally, the gentleman approached Etsuko and asked politely: "I wonder if you can tell me where we turn off this road to get to the Okamachi station of the Hankyu line."

As Etsuko told them about the shortcut through the ricefields and the government housing, the parents gaped in amazement at her precise Tokyo Yamate speech. The four children soon crowded about and looked up at Etsuko. A boy, about seven, quietly extended his closed fist before her. Then he relaxed his fingers just a little and said: "Look!"

In the cage made by his little fingers the bent light-green

body of a grasshopper was visible. In the shadow of the fingers the insect slowly extended and retracted its legs.

The oldest girl smartly slapped the boy's hand from below. He released the grasshopper, which flew clear, hopped twice on the ground, and plunged into the bushes on the side of the road and disappeared.

A brother-sister quarrel ensued, quelled by laughing parents. All nodded respectfully to Etsuko; then they took up their leisurely procession again, and stepped onto the grassy path between the ricefields.

Etsuko suddenly wondered whether the automobile so long awaited by the Sugimoto family had come up. She turned and looked up the highway, but again, as far as she could see, no car was visible. Shadows were accumulating gradually on the road surface; it was twilight.

It was bedtime, and the guests had not arrived. The household was beaten down by a heavy, oppressive mood; yet, taking their lead from the silent, irritable Yakichi, they had no choice save to act as if the visit would still take place.

Since Etsuko had come, nothing had brought the family together in anticipation comparable to this. Yakichi didn't say a word about the Equinox—he seemed to have forgotten it. He waited. Then he went on waiting. He was torn alternately by hope and disappointment. His demeanor was like that of Etsuko waiting for her husband to come home—hopeless and abandoned.

"He's still coming; it will work out"—it is horrible to say these words. After you say them it seems to you that, really, no one is coming.

Even Etsuko, who knew how Yakichi felt, could not believe that the hopes he had been filled with all day were simply hopes for worldly advancement. We are not wounded so deeply when betrayed by the things we hope for as when betrayed by things we try our best to despise. In such betrayal comes the dagger in the back.

Yakichi was sorry that he had shown the telegram to the union executive. Thanks to this he had given those people the opportunity to pin on him the label of a man cast aside. The executive insisted that he wanted to take just one quick look at the minister's face, and he hung around the Sugimoto home until about eight p.m., diligently helping wherever he could. Thus he saw everything: Yakichi's concern, Kensuke's half-teasing verbal digs, the whole family's preparations for a concerted welcome, the approaching night, the misgivings, the first definite signs of waning hope.

As for Etsuko, the events of this day taught her the lesson that it never pays to anticipate anything. At the same time she experienced, in response to Yakichi's painful efforts not to be wounded by this betrayal of his hopes, a strange stirring of affection that she had not known before in the time she had been in Maidemmura. The telegram might well have been dashed off by one of Yakichi's many cronies in the Osaka area as a practical joke dreamed up at some drunken party.

Etsuko treated Yakichi with unobtrusive gentleness, quietly intimate, mindful of his sensitivity to anything like sympathy.

After ten, Yakichi, his spirits crushed, for the first time thought about Ryosuke with a humiliating feeling of fear. A sense of sin that he had never once in his life entertained now lightly touched a corner of his heart. This sense grew heavier; it imparted a bittersweet taste to his tongue; it seemed to him a feeling that could grow upon one, cajoling the heart as one pondered it. The evidence for it was Etsuko, who this evening seemed more beautiful than ever.

"We bustled the Equinox away, didn't we? How would you like to go with me to the cemetery in Tokyo tomorrow?" he asked.

"Would you take me?" said Etsuko, her voice filled with something like joy. After a moment she went on: "Father, don't be concerned about Ryosuke. Even when he was living, he wasn't mine."

Two rain-filled days followed. The third day, September twenty-sixth, was fair. Everyone was busy from early morning with the laundry that had piled up.

As Etsuko hung up Yakichi's heavily darned socks to dry (he probably would be upset if Etsuko bought him new socks), she suddenly began to wonder what Saburo had done with the socks she had given him. This morning she had noticed that he was still wearing his torn sneakers over bare feet. That was when he said, with a smile that seemed to have grown in intimacy: "Ma'am, good morning." A small sore that might have been made by a grass cut peeped through a hole in the canvas over his grimy ankle.

I suppose he plans to wear them when he goes out. They weren't expensive at all, but that's the way a country boy would look at them.

Nevertheless, she had no way of asking him why he wasn't wearing them.

Lines had been stretched between the limbs of the four great pasania trees by the kitchen, and wash now took up every inch of the linen cords that webbed the trees together. The west wind blowing out of the chestnut forest made it flap and flutter. Maggie, tied beneath the lines, kept running back and forth under the white shapes sportively flapping over her head and every once in a while let out a prolonged howl. When the wash was hung, Etsuko walked around between the lines. As she did so a sudden gust of wind caught a still-wet apron and snapped it forcefully against her face. It was a refreshing slap that set her cheek glowing.

Where was Saburo? When she closed her eyes, the wounded, dirty ankle she had seen this morning floated before her. His smallest quirk, his smile, his poverty, the disrepair of his clothing—all of them struck her. His lovely poverty! That above all drew her. In Etsuko's eyes his poverty played the fetching role usually portrayed by shyness in a girl. "Maybe he is in his room, quietly absorbed in a samurai tale."

Etsuko crossed the kitchen, drying her hands on her apron. Beside the back door stood a waste container. It was a large can into which Miyo threw uneaten fish and discarded vegetables. When it was full, she would throw it in the trench where they made compost.

Something in the can caught Etsuko's eye; she stopped beside it. Out from under the yellowed vegetables and the fishbones a piece of brand-new fabric shone. It was a blue color she had seen before. She gingerly plunged in her fingers and pulled out the cloth. It was the socks. Under the blue pair, the brown pair came to light. She judged by their shape that they had not even been tried on. The price tag of the department store still hung to them by its staple.

She stood idly for a moment face-to-face with this perplexing discovery. The socks fell from her fingers and draped themselves over the fishy garbage. After two or three minutes, she looked around her, and then, as a mother might bury a fetus, she quickly buried the two pairs of socks under the yellowed greens and the fishbones. She washed her hands. As she washed them, and as she carefully dried them again on her apron, she went on pondering. It was not easy for her to get her thoughts in order. Before she succeeded in doing so, an unreasoning anger came over her and determined how she would act.

Saburo was in his three-mat room, changing into his work clothes. When he saw Etsuko appear between himself and the bay window, he dropped to a polite sitting posture and resumed buttoning his shirt. His sleeves were still unbuttoned. He glanced quickly at Etsuko's face. She still had not said a word. He buttoned his sleeves and sat silent. Saburo was struck by her expression, which had not changed in the slightest degree.

"What about the socks I gave you the other day? Would you show them to me?"

Etsuko said this gently, but someone hearing it could catch in the softness an unnecessarily menacing note. She was angry. It was an anger whose reasons were inexplicable, born by chance in some corner of her emotions; Etsuko blew it up, amplified it. If she had not, she couldn't have asked the questions she had in mind; her anger was born from the demands of the moment, a truly abstract emotion.

There was a movement in Saburo's black puppy's eyes. He unbuttoned his left sleeve and buttoned it again. Now it was his turn to be silent.

"What's the matter? Why don't you answer?"

She leaned her arm against the railing of the window. Then she looked mockingly at Saburo. Even in her anger, she savored this joy moment after moment. What a thing it was! Until now she had never imagined this. Indulging herself with this proudly victorious feeling. Observing this tanned, downward-inclined neck, this refreshingly shaven beard. Etsuko was not aware that her words were charged with caressing tones.

"It's all right. Don't be so crestfallen. I saw them, that's all—thrown away in the garbage can. Did you throw them there?"

"Yes, I did."

Saburo answered without hesitation. His answer unsettled Etsuko.

He's protecting someone, she thought. *If not he would have hesitated just a little.*

Suddenly Etsuko heard the sound of sobbing behind her. It was Miyo, crying into the skirt of an old gray serge apron far too long for her. Out of her sobs haltingly came the words: "I threw them away. I threw them away."

"What are you saying? What are you crying about?" As Etsuko pronounced these words, she glanced at Saburo's face. His eyes were filled with anxiety, with the wish to communicate with Miyo, in reaction to which Etsuko tore the apron from the girl's face with a brusqueness verging on cruelty.

Miyo's frightened, beet-red face was revealed. It was an ordinary country-girl face. There was something ugly about her tear-stained features: her cheeks like ripe persimmons, swollen and red, looking as if they would bruise if pressed; her thin eyebrows; her large, stolid, unexpressive eyes; her impossible nose. Only her lips unsettled Etsuko slightly. Etsuko's lips were rather thin. Quivering with sobs, wet and shining with tears and saliva, these lips had just the right degree of roundness, like a pretty red pincushion.

"Well, why? I'm not particularly worried about the socks being thrown away. I just don't understand—that's why I'm asking."

"Yes, ma'am—"

Saburo interrupted her. His glib speech made his normal self look like fraud: "Actually, it was I who threw them away, ma'am. They seemed much too fine for me to wear, so I threw them away, ma'am."

"Don't say such silly things; it won't work," said Etsuko. Miyo feared that Saburo's actions would be reported to Yakichi, who would then certainly punish him. She could not allow him to protect her as he had been doing any longer. So she went on before Saburo could say any more: "I threw them away, ma'am. Right after you gave them to Saburo, he showed them to me. I was awfully suspicious and said you didn't give them to him for nothing. Then he got mad and said, 'All right, you keep them,' and stalked off leaving them behind. Then I threw them away—women can't wear men's socks, after all."

Again Miyo pulled the apron over her face. What she had said made sense—if one ignored that ingratiating white lie: "Women can't wear men's socks."

Etsuko understood one thing now, and as a result she said resignedly: "It's all right. Don't cry. If Chieko and the rest see you, I don't know what they'll think. There's no reason to make such a fuss about a pair or two of socks. Now, calm down. Dry your tears."

She deliberately avoided looking at Saburo, put her arm around Miyo's shoulder and led her outside. She studied the shoulder she was embracing, the slightly dirty neck, and the unkempt coiffure.

A woman like this! Of all things! A woman like this!

Through the row of pasania trees the fresh autumn sky gleamed; from it came the screams of shrikes, in voice for the first time this year. Miyo heard them and walked into a puddle, remnant of the recent rains, splashing muddy water on Etsuko's dress. "Aaaa . . ." Etsuko said, and let go of the girl.

Miyo suddenly dropped to the ground like a dog and carefully wiped Etsuko's skirt, using the same serge apron with which she had just dried her tears.

This wordless display of devotion was, in the eyes of Etsuko, standing there wordlessly permitting it, not so much a touching country-girl wile, as something charged with courteous, sullen hostility.

One day after that Saburo, wearing the socks, bowed to Etsuko as if nothing had happened and innocently smiled.

* * * *

Etsuko now had a reason for living.

From that day until the unpleasant incident of the October tenth Autumn Festival she had something to live for.

Etsuko had never asked for salvation. As a result, it was strange that a reason for living should have been born to her.

It is easy enough for people to see life as valueless. In fact, people with any degree of sensitivity have difficulty forgetting it. Etsuko's instinct in these matters was strikingly like that of the hunter. If in the distant wood she should chance to see the white tail of a hare, her cunning would come into play, all the blood of her body would grow turbulent, her sinews would surge, her nervous system would grow taut and concentrate itself like an arrow in flight. In the leisurely days when she lacked this reason for living she was like quite a different hunter, passing indolent days and nights asking no more than a sleep by the fire.

To some people living is extremely simple; to others, it is extremely difficult. Against this unjust imbalance, more striking than the injustice of racial discrimination, Etsuko felt not the slightest rancor.

It's best to take life lightly, she thought. *After all, people to whom living is easy don't have to give any excuse for living beyond that. Those who find it hard, though, very quickly use something more than just living as an excuse. Saying life is hard is nothing to brag about. The power we have to find all the difficulties in life helps to make life easy for the majority of men. If we didn't have that power, life would be something without simplicity or difficulty—a slippery, empty sphere without a foothold.*

This power is one that prevents life from looking like that, a power that people who never come to see life thus do not know. Yet it is not anything out of the ordinary as powers go; in fact it is nothing more than an everyday necessity. He who tampers with the scales of life and makes it seem unduly heavy will receive his punishment in hell. Even if life's weight is not tampered with, it is like a coat, its weight barely noticed; only the sick man feels the weight of that overcoat and grows stiff in the shoulders. I have to wear heavier clothing than others, she thought, *because it happens that my soul was born and still lives in the snow country. The problems of life are to me nothing but the suit of armor that protects me.*

Her reason for living made tomorrow, the day after tomorrow, and whatever the future might bring seem not at all heavy. They were still heavy, to be sure, but some subtle shift in her center of gravity sent Etsuko blithely and buoyantly into the future. Was it hope? Never.

All day she monitored what Saburo and Miyo were doing. It would gain her nothing but pain to discover them kissing under some tree, or to discover in the middle of the night some thread connecting their widely separated rooms. Since, however, uncertainty would bring her even greater pain, Etsuko was determined to stoop to any action that would enable her to search out proof of their love.

Judged merely by its end result, her passion was shockingly authentic evidence of the limitlessness of the human passion for self-torture. A passion lavishly expended in the destruction of her hopes alone, it was a scale model of human existence—perhaps streamlined, perhaps vaulted. Passions do have a form, and through their forms become biological cultures in which human lives can be fully displayed.

Nobody noticed, Etsuko felt, how she watched the other two everywhere they went. She was perfectly calm, and worked harder than usual.

Etsuko inspected the rooms of Miyo and Saburo while they were out, much as Yakichi had once done with her room. No evidence, however, came to light. This pair was not the diary-writing kind. They didn't know how to write love notes; nor were they even aware of that gentle conspiracy of love in which the present moment seems to stand forth already endowed with the beauty of reminiscence. With these two there was neither evidence nor commemoration. When they met, surely, there was only a mingling of glances . . . of hands . . . of lips . . . of breasts. And after that, perhaps this here and that there . . . Ah! How easy! How simple, beautiful, abstract an action!

Words unneeded, meaning unnecessary; an attitude like that of an athlete throwing a javelin; a stance necessary and adequate to the simple tasks for which it was assumed. That action . . . that behavior that seemed to have been assumed entirely to conform with that simple, abstract, beautiful line—and of that behavior not one shred of evidence remained. It was an action like that of a swallow flying for a moment above the surface of the plain.

Etsuko's dreams veered at times, and at one moment her existence seemed to be carried away into the darkness of outer space in one great swing of a beautiful cradle, turbulently tossed on a gleaming column of water.

In Miyo's room, Etsuko found a cheap mirror in a celluloid frame, a red comb, cheap cold cream, Mentholatum, just one half-decent kimono of cheap, Chichibu *meisen*, arrow-feather fabric, some badly wrinkled sashes, a brand-new petticoat, a shapeless bag of a dress for summer wear and the slip that went with it (in the summer Miyo blithely went shopping in the village wearing only these two garments), an old women's magazine with pages thumbed till they looked like dirty artificial flowers, a maudlin letter from a friend in the country, and, on closer inspection, clinging to all, strands of reddish hair.

In Saburo's room, Etsuko saw nothing but the essentials of an even plainer way of life.

Are they, I wonder, being as circumspect in avoiding my search as I am being diligent in seeking them out? Or am I in my careful scrutiny missing what I seek because it is inserted, as in the Poe story I borrowed from Kensuke, in some letter rack out in plain sight?

As Etsuko left the room she met Yakichi coming toward her down the hall. Since the hall ended with Miyo's room Yakichi had no business coming down it unless he was going there.

"You, here?" Yakichi said.

"Yes."

Etsuko's reply was not apologetic. As they went back to Yakichi's room the old man's body bumped clumsily against her. Not at all because the hallway was too narrow. His body struck hers for no reason, as would the body of a sulky child pulled along by his mother.

When they had settled down in the room, Yakichi said: "Why were you there in his room?"

"I went to look at his diary."

Yakichi's mouth moved indistinctly. He said nothing more.

* * * *

The tenth of October was Autumn Festival day in the several neighboring villages. Saburo had dressed and left with the members of the Young Men's League before sundown. The festival was so crowded that it was perilous to take small children on foot. The best way to restrain the supplications of Nobuko and Natsuo to go along, therefore, seemed to be to ask them to stay with their mother to mind the house. After supper, Yakichi, Etsuko, Kensuke and Chieko, along with Miyo, went off to the local shrine and the village festival.

The great drums had been booming near and far since sundown. Something in the wind, like screams, like songs, sounded with them. These noises that flowed piercingly over the ricefields in the dark night, noises like the songs of birds and animals crying together in the night, did not disturb the stillness; in fact, they deepened it. Country nights, even in areas not far from great cities, are deep like that, broken only here and there with the cries of insects.

For a time after they had finished getting ready to go to the festival, Kensuke and Chieko had opened the windows and listened to the sound of the drums coming from all directions. "That must be the one at the Hachiman shrine by the station. That must be the one at the village shrine we're going to. That, I think, is the drum at the village hall over there, the drum they let little children—their noses daubed with white powder—take turns beating on. Its sound is the most youthful; at times it stops altogether . . ."

They were so lost in the joy of this guessing game, so puerile in the differing opinions that brought them to the verge of quarreling, that they sounded as though they were taking part in a play. It was hard to believe their conversation was carried out by a husband of thirty-eight and a wife of thirty-seven.

"No, that's from the direction of Okamachi—from the Hachiman shrine by the station."

"My, you're stubborn. Here you've been living in this neighborhood for six years, and you still don't know where the station is from here."

"All right, would you be so kind as to bring me a map and a compass?"

"Why, madam, we don't have things like that here."

"Yes, I'm the madam, and you're the plain old man of the house."

"Of course. And it isn't everybody that can become the wife of a plain old man of the house. Why, all the ordinary wives of the world are Mrs. Department Heads, Mrs. Fishmongers, Mrs. Trumpeters. You were born lucky. As wife to a plain old man of the house, you are the paragon of wifely success. As a female, you can take over the life of a male. Surely, there is no greater success for a female, is there?"

"You don't have it quite straight. I meant you were a plain, ordinary man of the house."

"Ordinary? Wonderful! The highest point at which human life and art meet is in the ordinary. To look down on the ordinary is to despise what you can't have. Show me a man who fears being ordinary, and I'll show you a man who is not yet a man. The earliest days of the *haiku,* before Basho, before Shiki, were filled with the vigor of an age in which the spirit of the ordinary had not died."

"Yes, and your *haiku* show the ordinary at its highest point of development."

Through the tone of this, through this shallow dialogue, ran everlastingly the same theme—the theme of Chieko's boundless respect for her husband's "learning." Among the Tokyo intellectuals of a decade ago, couples like this were not at all uncommon. In their respectful pursuit of the forms of the grand tradition even into this time, however, they were like a woman wearing last year's hairdo among country folk, as if it were still the mode.

Kensuke lit a cigarette and leaned against the window frame. The smoke he exhaled streamed on the night air like white hair floating on water, entangling itself in the branches of the persimmon tree nearby. After a short silence he said: "Father isn't ready yet, is he?"

"It's Etsuko who isn't ready. Father may be helping her tie her sash. I know it's hard to believe, but he even ties the string of her petticoat for her. Whenever she dresses, they close the door of her room tight and talk in low tones, so you can't tell how long . . ."

"Father's really living it up in his last years, isn't he?"

Their conversation naturally swung around to the subject of Saburo. Etsuko's calm comportment of recent days, they finally decided, must be evidence that she had given him up. Rumor sometimes follows a more precise logic than fact, and fact more than rumor is apt to have a lie in it somewhere.

The way to the village shrine led through the woods behind the house. Not far from the pine grove by which they had gone cherry-blossom viewing this spring, they came to a fork in the path. They took the fork that led away from the pine grove. For a while there was only swampland covered with rushes and water chestnuts. They descended a steep hill with a cluster of houses at the bottom. On the mountain across the valley lay the village shrine.

Miyo was in front, carrying a paper lantern. Kensuke walked behind, illuminating the path with a flashlight. At the fork in the path they were joined by Tanaka, a rugged, honest farmer, also on his way to the festival. He carried a flute, on which he practiced as they walked. His playing was surprisingly skillful, but his cheerful tunes somehow struck them as sad, rendering their procession led by its paper lantern as silent as a funeral. To liven things up Kensuke started clapping his hands to each tune; everyone joined him. The sound of their clapping came back in hollow echoes from the surface of the swamp.

"It's odd, isn't it," said Yakichi; "the sound of the drum seems farther away here."

"It's the terrain that does that," said Kensuke, from the rear.

At that moment Miyo stumbled and almost fell, an occurrence which prompted Kensuke to take her paper lantern and her place at the head of the line. There was no need to have this witless girl conduct them.

Etsuko stood beside the path where she had stepped aside to make way for Kensuke and watched the lantern change hands. In the lantern light Miyo's skin seemed rather green. There was no light in her eyes. In fact, she even seemed to be having trouble breathing.

This was the way Etsuko's eyes had now learned to observe things—in that instant when the paper lantern was passed from hand to hand and lighted the upper half of Miyo's body—in appraisals that brief.

But that glimpse was soon forgotten, as the great festival lanterns hanging from the eaves of houses brought exclamations of admiration from the little column toiling up the slope.

Most of the villagers had gone to the festival, leaving

only the great lanterns to guard their homes, bright and silent. The Sugimoto group crossed the stone bridge over the creek that flowed through the town. The geese that swam in the creek in the daytime cried out from their coops as the noisy strangers passed. "Just like babies crying at night," said Yakichi. Everyone laughed. They were thinking of Natsuo and his negligent mother.

Etsuko looked at Miyo in her arrow-feather kimono, careful that no gleam of ill will escaped from her eyes. She wasn't concerned about what the family might see. It was Miyo she was concerned about. Just the surmise—surmise, nothing more—that Miyo, this dull-witted country maiden, so much as suspected her jealousy, would be more than Etsuko's self-respect could stand. Whether it was Miyo's complexion or her kimono, Etsuko could not tell, but somehow this evening the girl was more than a little beautiful.

It's a strange world, Etsuko thought. *When I was a child, it was unthinkable for a maid to go around in anything but a striped kimono. When the likes of servants can go about in stylish fabrics, tradition can't stand, society's order is being spat upon. If my mother had anything to do with her, she'd fire her before the day was over.*

No matter how one looks at it, from below or above, status is a fine substitute for jealousy. What better evidence for this could there be than that Etsuko never harbored a bit of that old-time social consciousness in her attitude toward Saburo?

Etsuko wore a scattered-chrysanthemum silk kimono, of a kind rare outside the city, under a shiny black *haori,* tailored slightly short. The scent of her treasured Houbigant wafted faintly about her—a cologne that had no place at a country festival, obviously put on for Saburo alone. The unsuspecting Yakichi himself had sprayed it on her neck. On downy hair the color of her skin, infinitesimally small droplets of cologne rested, shining like pearls, incomparably lovely. Her skin had always been smooth; there was, in fact, a definite contradiction between the opulent area here entrusted to Yakichi, and the horny and soil-encrusted flesh of his hand. Yet his dirty hand would gradually eliminate all boundaries and merge with her fragrant bosom. In the process of fashioning this artificial contradiction, Yakichi seemed to find himself drawn for the first time into the restful sense that he really possessed her.

As they turned into a lane by the rice distribution center, they were suddenly greeted by the stench of an acetylene lamp, in the light of which they saw at last the evening bustle of hucksters. One was selling candy. Another was selling toy pinwheels—the handles of them impaled in a bale of straw. Another was selling flowery paper umbrellas. Near him others were selling—though it was not the season—firecrackers, children's card games, and balloons.

In the festival season these merchants would go to the Osaka candy stalls and buy leftover goods at reduced prices. Then they would loiter around the Hankyu Umeda station and ask passers-by what station stop was celebrating a festival today. If they went first to the Hachiman shrine by the Okamachi station and saw competitors already installed there, they would proceed to this second-choice festival. Their dreams of great markups almost gone, they would arrive in small groups from across the fields, their gait testifying to their resignation. Many of the peddlers here this evening were old men and women.

The children were gathered in a knot about some little toy cars that ran around in a circle. The Sugimoto family passed the peddlers one by one, debating whether to buy Natsuo a fifty-yen auto.

"It's too high, too high. Have Etsuko buy him one the next time she goes to Osaka; it will be much cheaper," said Yakichi. "Besides, all they sell in places like this are things you buy today and find broken tomorrow."

His denunciation was handed down in a loud voice, and the old man selling toys glared at him fiercely. Yakichi glared back.

Yakichi won. The old man turned away and resumed his patter with the children around him. Childishly drunk with victory, Yakichi passed through a *torii* and started up the stone steps.

To be sure, Maidemmura's prices were higher than those of Osaka. They only bought in Maidemmura what was absolutely necessary. Take the night soil for instance. "Osaka honey has a good price," the saying went, and in winter it sold for two thousand yen a cartload. Farmers went to Osaka and purchased it, and Yakichi bought it with a sour face. In the materials that went into it alone, he said, Osaka's night soil was better than what was produced here.

As they started up the stairs a sound like thundering surf descended upon them. The sky above the stairway filled with dancing sparks; the sound of splitting bamboo mixed with shouts of wonder beat upon their eardrums. The limbs of an old cypress tree stood out naked in the cruel light of blazing bonfires.

"If we start up from here, I don't think we'll ever get to the shrine," said Kensuke.

With that their column swung away from the stairway, which they had climbed halfway, and took the path that wound its way to the back of the main shrine. It was Miyo and not Yakichi who was out of breath when they reached their objective. With her big hands she uneasily rubbed her colorless cheeks.

The front of the shrine sanctuary was like the bridge of a battleship directing its bow into a roaring swirl of fire and tumult. The women, who dared not enter the swirl, stood above and looked down on the pandemonium in the courtyard, from which the stone staircase and wall barely protected them. They were silent with good reason, for over their heads, and over the stairs, and over their hands that gripped the stone barrier, the shadows cast by the fire and the shadows of the men that stood between them and the fire swung madly about.

At times the bonfires would pick up force tremendously; the flames would seem to be infusing themselves with energy. The faces of the women spectators—joined by this time by the Sugimoto family—would be etched in stark reflections; the cord that ran to the bell-pull hanging from the eaves of the shrine would shine as red as if struck by the setting sun. Then the shadows would leap as if dancing, licking up that moment's brightness, leaving the group on the top of the stairs black, silent, and peevish.

"Surely they've gone mad, and Saburo right along with them," said Kensuke as if to himself, staring down at the writhing mass below them. He glanced toward Etsuko, beside him, and noticed that the side of her *haori* was ripped, a fact she seemed unaware of. She seemed to him strangely appealing this evening.

"Oh, Etsuko, your *haori* is ripped," he called. He had a penchant for saying what didn't need saying.

At this moment a new note came into the shouting. The useless message from Kensuke never reached Etsuko's ear. In the harsh glare of the bonfires her profile seemed slightly sterner than usual, slightly more majestic, and slightly crueler.

The mob in the courtyard was constantly rushing to one or another of the three *torii* and jamming together there. Their movements, which at first glance seemed to have no special order, were directed by a great lion's head held high over them. Opening and closing his jaws, his green mane streaming behind, the lion's head floated about as if cleaving the waves. It was manipulated at different times by three young men clad in cotton kimonos, forced to give way to each other after only short stints, so overwhelming was the perspiration induced by the chore.

Over a hundred young men followed the lion, each carrying a white paper lantern. They would crowd around the lion and jostle against each other, striking their lanterns together. After a time the lion, as if carried away by rage, would break free and rush toward another *torii*. Again the young men would follow, and again they would hold up their lanterns, some miraculously still alight, their owners frequently unaware that all had been broken save the handle. And all the while they shouted at the top of their lungs.

In the center of the courtyard bamboo poles had been erected. When the base of each pole was lighted, the entire pole quickly ignited and exploded. As each blazing pole fell, another was erected in its place. Compared with these mad torches, the bonfires at the four corners of the courtyard were fairly tranquil exercises in pyrotechnics.

These village dwellers, who on an ordinary day would have nothing to do with danger, were here braving the flying sparks and crowding about tirelessly, watching the extraordinary impulsive movements of the massed young men following the lion. Outwardly the spectators were calm, but in their ranks a certain undulant cohesion seethed, creating collisions that threatened at any moment to catapult the front row of viewers into the turbulent sea of young men. Older men carrying fans, who were responsible for keeping everything within bounds, moved between the young men and the spectators, shouting themselves hoarse, alternately inciting the one group and restraining the other.

The whole scene, as viewed from the top of the stone steps of the sanctuary, seemed like the form of a great dusky snake, writhing about the flaming poles, throwing off phosphorescence in all directions.

Etsuko's eyes were riveted to the area where the paper lanterns crashed together so fiercely. In her mind, Yakichi, Kensuke, and even Miyo no longer existed. The embodiment of this outcry, this frenzy, this completely demented demonstration—in the hazy drunkenness of Etsuko's perceptions—was Saburo. It had to be Saburo, she thought.

This swirling, needless waste of life's energies seemed to Etsuko virtually a shining thing; her consciousness seemed to float on this perilous confusion, melting like a piece of ice on a baking pan. She could feel her face light up every once in a while in the glare of the flaming poles and the bonfires. She irrelevantly recalled the profusion of November sunshine that fell on her like an avalanche as they opened the door to carry out her husband's coffin.

Chieko realized that Etsuko was looking for Saburo. It would never have occurred to her that her sister-in-law might be looking for something more. Out of her native kindness, Chieko said: "My, it's exciting. But I'd like to go down there. Here you can't really feel how savage a country festival can be."

Kensuke caught his wife's wink and along with it the motive behind her suggestion. He knew too that Yakichi dared not come along. That provided him with a second motive, that of staging a small vendetta against his father.

"All right. Get set! Let's go! Do you want to go, Etsuko? You're young enough."

Yakichi put on his usual sour face. It was the proud, sour face of a man accustomed to manipulating others with just a slight change of expression. There had been a time when just one such look would have been enough to make an executive tender his resignation. Etsuko, however, didn't look at him, and quickly said: "All right. I'll go along."

"Father?" asked Chieko. Yakichi didn't answer and turned his sour look on Miyo, making it clear to her that she was to remain here with her employer.

"I'll wait here; come back soon," he said to Etsuko, without looking at her.

Etsuko, Kensuke, and Chieko linked hands, descended the stone stairs, and walked into the noisy throng as if wading into the surf. The spectators down here moved about more easily than they had seemed to when viewed from above. One had no trouble cutting past all the spiritless, gaping faces and moving to the front.

Etsuko heard the bamboo exploding at her side and felt refreshed. Any unpleasant sound would have come pleasantly to her ears now. These delicate ears of hers, no longer moved by trifles, asking only for the risk of being strained to bursting, must really have been listening intently to the rhythm of some emotion dwelling deep inside her.

Suddenly, above their heads, its mane streaming, went the lion's head, its golden teeth exposed, moving toward another *torii*. Pandemonium ensued, as human beings flowed in waves to right and left. Something dazzling cut across Etsuko's line of vision. It was a band of half-naked young men moving as one in the glare of the flames. Some wore their hair loose and disheveled; some wore white headbands tied so the ends streamed behind. Emitting animal-like shouts, they churned past Etsuko, filling the breeze with musky odor. As they passed, the dark reverberation of hard flesh striking hard flesh, the bright squeal of sweaty skin clinging to and breaking away from sweaty skin filled the air. So entangled were their legs in the darkness that they looked like some meaninglessly entangled mass of inhuman creatures. It seemed as if not one of them could know which legs were his own.

"I wonder where Saburo is," said Kensuke. "When they're naked, you can't tell one from the other."

He was taking no chances on losing one of the women, and had his arm around each of them. Etsuko's slippery shoulder threatened at any moment to slide from his grasp.

"It's true," he said, agreeing with himself. "When people are naked you can really understand why human individuality is such a fragile thing. And when it comes to thinking, there are just four kinds; that's all: the thinking of a fat man, the thinking of a skinny man, the thinking of a tall, gangly man, and the thinking of a little man. When it comes to faces, now—whatever ones you look at—they never have more than two eyes, one nose, and one mouth apiece. You don't see anyone with one eye.

"Take even the most individualistic face—all it's good for is to symbolize the difference between its owner and other people. What's love? Nothing more than symbol falling for symbol. And when it comes to sex—that's anonymity falling for anonymity. Chaos and chaos, the unisexual mating of depersonalization with depersonalization. Masculinity? Femininity? You can't tell the difference. See, Chieko?"

Even Chieko looked bored; she grunted agreement.

Etsuko couldn't help laughing. *This man's thinking—constantly, almost incontinently, mumbling in the ear. That's it! It's "cerebral incontinence!" What pitiful pants-wetting! This man's thoughts are as ridiculous as his backside.*

The real absurdity, though, is that what he is saying is so out of tempo with all the shouting, all the excitement, all the smells, all the activity, all the life around him here. If he were a musician, no conductor would have him in his orchestra. But what can you do with a country orchestra except recognize it's out of tune and make do?"

Etsuko opened her eyes wide. Her shoulder slid ever so gently out of Kensuke's sticky hand. She had found Saburo. His usually taciturn lips were open wide—shouting. His sharp teeth showed white and shining, sparkling in the light of the bonfires.

In his eyes—never turned toward her—Etsuko saw another glowing resplendent bonfire.

Again the lion's head stood out above the crowd, seeming to survey the entire scene. Then it capriciously changed direction and headed straight into the spectators, green mane floating proudly, moving toward the main *torii* at the front of the shrine. A band of half-naked young men thundered behind.

Etsuko relinquished all power over her legs and followed the procession. Behind her she could hear Kensuke call, "Etsuko! Etsuko!" and the shrill laughter of Chieko. She did not look back. Something inside her seemed to stand forth out of a vague, mushy quagmire and to flash forward with almost herculean, physical power.

On certain occasions human beings are imbued with the belief that they can accomplish anything. In such moments they seem to glimpse much that is normally invisible to human eyes. Then, later, even after they have sunk to the bottom of memory's well, these moments sometimes revive and again suggest to men the miraculous plenitude of the world's pains and joys. None can avoid these moments of destiny; nor can anyone—no matter who he is—avoid the misfortune of seeing more than his eyes can take in.

Etsuko now felt she could do anything. Her cheeks burned like fire. Jostled by the expressionless throng, she sped, half-stumbling, toward the front *torii*. The fan of a marshal struck her on the breast, but she did not feel the blow. She was caught in a fierce clash of torpor and frenzy.

Saburo was not conscious of her proximity. His marvelously fleshed, lightly tanned back was turned to the pushing spectators. His face was turned toward the lion in the center, shouting at it, challenging it. He held his lantern, no longer lighted though unmarred by the rents and punctures that disfigured the others, high with his lithe arm. The ceaselessly twisting lower half of his body was lost in darkness, but his barely moving back was given over to a mad kaleidoscope of flame and shadow. The movements of the flesh around his shoving shoulder bones seemed like the exertions of the wings of a powerful bird in flight.

Etsuko longed to touch him with her fingers. What kind of desire this was she did not know. That back was to her metaphorically a bottomless ocean depth; she longed to throw herself into it. Her desire was close to that of the person who drowns himself; he does not necessarily covet death so much as what comes after the drowning—something different from what he had before, at the least a different world.

Another strong, wavelike motion in the throng impelled everyone forward. The half-naked youths moved counter to this, backing up in concert with the capricious lion's head. Etsuko stumbled forward, pushed by the throng, and collided with a bare back, warm as fire, coming from the opposite direction. She reached out her hands and held it off. It was Saburo's back. She savored the touch of his flesh. She savored the majestic warmth of him.

The mob behind her pushed again, causing her fingernails to gouge into Saburo's back. He did not even feel it. In all the mad pushing and shoving he had no idea what woman was pressing against his back. Etsuko felt his blood dripping between her fingers.

The marshals didn't seem to have the crowd very much under control. The mad young men banded together in one mass and, shouting all the while, moved close to one brightly blazing bamboo pole. Embers fell before their feet and were trampled upon. The barefoot men were past feeling the heat of them. The pole stood wrapped in fire, lighting up the limbs of the old cypress tree with flame and scarlet smoke. The burning bamboo leaves were yellow, as if caught by sunlight. The slim fiery pillar shook and exploded, then dipped deep from side to side like a sailboat mast, and suddenly toppled into the middle of the jostling crowd.

Etsuko thought she saw a woman with her hair afire laughing loudly. That was about all she remembered with any clarity. Somehow she got away, and found herself standing by the stone steps in front of the shrine. She later recalled a moment when all the sky she could see was filled with sparks. Yet she felt no sense of horror. The young men were struggling again to plunge toward another *torii*. The spectators seemed to have forgotten their fear of a few minutes ago and were streaming after them as before. Nothing had happened.

Etsuko wasn't sure how she had found her way here. She stood in the courtyard of the shrine, staring vacantly at the diagonal pattern thrown on the ground by the flames and the human shadows. Then she felt a rough blow at her shoulder. It was Kensuke's sticky hand.

"Here you are, Etsuko. We were worried sick about you."

Etsuko looked at him silently, showing no emotion. He, however, went on breathlessly: "Something's happened. Come with me."

"Is anything wrong?"

"Never mind. Come with me."

Kensuke took her hand and mounted the staircase with great strides. There was a circle of people around the spot where they had left Yakichi and Miyo. Kensuke elbowed people aside and conducted Etsuko into the circle.

Miyo was lying face-up on two benches that had been brought together. Chieko was leaning over her, trying to loosen her sash. Yakichi was standing by awkwardly. So carelessly was Miyo dressed that the skin of her bosom showed through her loosened clothing. She lay unconscious, her mouth slightly opened. Her hand hung down, seemingly twisted, her fingernails striking the paving stones.

"What happened?"

"She just fainted. It looks like cerebral ischemia, or something. Maybe it's an epileptic fit."

"We'd better call a doctor."

"Tanaka just called one. He's coming with a stretcher."

"Should we let Saburo know?"

"It's all right. It doesn't seem to be serious."

Kensuke could not bear to look at Miyo's face, green as grass, but directed his eyes in the opposite direction. He was one of those men who, as they say, can't kill a flea.

The stretcher arrived shortly and was picked up by Tanaka and one of the members of the Young Men's League. Kensuke led the way slowly down the perilous stone stairway, lighting the way around the twists and turns with his flashlight. In the illumination of the flashlight Miyo's face, with its tightly closed eyes, looked like a *noh* mask, making the children who came up alongside scream in mock fright.

Yakichi followed the stretcher mumbling something under his breath: "How humiliating! Who knows what people will say. She has to go and get sick right in the middle of the festival . . ."

Fortunately they didn't have to pass the street shops to get to the hospital. They carried the stretcher through a *torii*, traversed a dark twisting street, and entered the hospital. Even after the patient and her attendants had passed inside, however, a knot of the curious remained outside. The festival with its endless repetitions had begun to bore them; they wished to find out now how this new event would come out. Kicking the gravel, exchanging rumors, they waited happily for this not unusual by-product of the festival. It would fill the next ten days with entertaining conversation.

A young doctor had recently inherited the hospital. This arrogant boy genius found the country origins of his dead father and his entire line ridiculous, and villa dwellers like the Sugimotos made him uneasy. When they met on the street he would greet them with a solicitude seasoned with discomfiture—a discomfiture based on his fear they would see through the city-slicker patina he wore.

The patient was carried into the examination room. Yakichi, Etsuko, Kensuke, and Chieko were conducted into the parlor that faced the garden. They said little. Yakichi kept twitching his thick eyebrows as if to chase away a fly or blowing noisily into a cavity in one of his back teeth. He had lost his head, and he regretted it. If he hadn't called for Tanaka, all the fuss wouldn't have happened; they wouldn't have had to carry her on a stretcher, only the people nearby would have noticed, and that would have been that.

Once when he had gone into the union offices, one of the executives who had been telling a funny story interrupted his tale and said nothing more. It was the man who had come to the Sugimoto home the day the minister was supposed to arrive. If that had provided a good story, this evening's events would be much worse. It seemed perilously sure they would provide fuel for even more vicious surmises.

Etsuko was looking down at her hands, which were resting in her lap. On one nail she saw a drop of flame-colored blood, already dry. Almost unconsciously she lifted it to her lips.

The hospital director slid open the door and walked halfway in. He spoke to them as if proud of his acquaintance with the Sugimoto family and said, nonchalantly: "Not a thing to worry about; she's conscious again."

Yakichi found that report not worth comment and asked brusquely: "And what caused it?"

The doctor came into the room and closed the door. Then he pulled up his trouser legs by the crease and sat down clumsily beside them. He smirked unprofessionally as he said: "She's pregnant."

4

A *VISION* of the long-forgotten Ryosuke returned to haunt Etsuko's days, as he had disturbed her tortured rest the night following the festival. This vision, however, was not surrounded by a sentimental halo, as was that which appeared to her immediately after his death; it was a naked, vicious, evil visitation.

In this vision her life with him became transformed into endless lessons in a disreputable school set up in a secret room. Ryosuke didn't love Etsuko; he taught her. He didn't teach her; he trained her. He taught her tricks, the way peddlers train deformed girls.

Those detestable, perverted, cruel hours of instruction . . . those countless forced memorizations, those whips, those beatings . . . they all taught Etsuko the lesson: "If you can deny yourself jealousy, you can stop loving."

With all her power Etsuko strove to make this lesson her own—to no avail.

To stop loving—it was cruel tutelage, yet to conform

with it Etsuko would have endured any privation. But the lesson of that tutelage and the prescription for it were made useless by the lack of some essential ingredient.

She had come to Maidemmura seeking that ingredient and, to her relief, found it—alas, a clever imitation of a useless prescription. It was false, and the thing feared, the thing worried about, happened again.

As the doctor smirked and said, "She's pregnant," an excruciating pain struck Etsuko's breast. She felt the blood drain from her face; a terrible dryness in her mouth brought her close to retching. It would not do to have anyone notice! She watched the expressions of Yakichi, Kensuke, and Chieko, all alive with not simply unfeigned, but absolutely dumbfounded, expressions of surprise.

So that's it. This time we're surprised! I must act surprised, by all means.

"Oh, how awful. I can't believe it," said Chieko.

"Shocking, isn't it?" said Yakichi, trying to lighten the tone of the discussion, "but with girls the way they are nowadays . . ." He was trying to convey to the doctor that this affair was not of his doing. (The first thing that had occurred to him was how much it would cost to hush up the doctor and the nurse.)

"Are you surprised, Etsuko?" said Chieko.

"Yes," said Etsuko, smiling stiffly.

"Nothing surprises you, cool as you are," said Chieko.

She was right. Etsuko wasn't surprised. She was jealous.

Kensuke and Chieko found this affair fascinating. They had no moral bias—that was their strong point, in which they took pride. Thanks to this self-styled strong point, however, they fell into the position of bystanders, devoid of all sense of justice. Everyone likes to watch a fire; but those who watch it from a terrace are no better than those who watch from the street.

Is there such a thing as a morality without bias? Their dream of a modern, ideal world helped them somehow to bear life in the country, and the only tool they had to build that dream, to make it real, was advice, the kind counsel on which they held the patent. Advising made this fine pair feel occupied—spiritually, at least. Spiritual busyness—in truth it was the world of the sick.

In Chieko's breast rang a boundless respect for the learning her husband carried so gracefully. After all, he didn't talk about it, but he could read Greek! That was, in Japan at least, a rare feat. He also knew Latin grammar to the extent of having memorized the paradigms of 217 verbs. He could recite the long names of all the characters in a great number of Russian novels. Not only that, but he could talk for hours on things such as how the Japanese *noh* play is one of the world's greatest "cultural legacies" (he loved that phrase) and how its "refined elegance is truly comparable with the great traditions of the West." Like an author who thinks himself a genius because his books don't sell, he felt that his not being asked to lecture anywhere was evidence that the world was not ready for his message.

This erudite couple was convinced that if they so much as extended a hand, humanity would be somehow transformed. A conviction maintained because it was never put into practice. As filled with conceit as the thinking of the retired soldier. It may well have been something Kensuke had inherited from the man he most despised, Yakichi Sugimoto.

Their advice had neither bias nor self-interest, so when

someone who should have followed it did not and ran into difficulty, they declared he had brought it on himself with his biases. They felt they could lay blame on anyone, and as a result they fell into the trap of having to excuse everyone too. As they saw it, nothing in this world was of real importance.

They felt that they could effortlessly change their lives by extending a hand ever so slightly, but it was too much trouble to do that right now. The difference between them and Etsuko was that their effortless love was expended on their own shiftlessness.

Thus, as Kensuke and Chieko walked home under a threatening sky late on the night of the festival, they were excited by their anticipation of the details of Miyo's pregnancy. Miyo was staying the night at the hospital and would not return until the next morning.

"There's no doubt whose child it is. It's Saburo's," said Kensuke.

"Certainly," said Chieko.

A rarely experienced sense of desolation gripped Kensuke at the thought that his wife did not suspect him in the slightest. It was a point on which he felt a jot of jealousy toward the dead philanderer Ryosuke.

"What if it was me?"

"Don't say such things! I can't stand indecent jokes."

Chieko put both hands to her ears, as would a child, swayed her hips wildly from side to side, and pouted. Earnest woman that she was, she detested vulgar humor.

"It's Saburo. It has to be."

Kensuke thought so too. Yakichi, after all, had lost all normal capacities. One had only to look at Etsuko to see that clearly.

"I wonder how this is going to work out. Etsuko doesn't look as if she's taking it very well." They watched the backs of Yakichi and Etsuko, walking together five or six paces ahead of them, and lowered their voices. Etsuko carried her shoulders as if she were angry. She was in the grip of some powerful emotion; that was clear. "The way she looks, she's still in love with Saburo."

"It must be hard on Etsuko. Why is it that she always has such bad luck?"

"Sometimes jiltings run in series—like miscarriages. Her nervous system has gotten in the habit of it, I suppose, and when she falls in love it has to end in miscarriage."

"But Etsuko is smart, and I think she'll get her feelings under control sooner or later."

"Let's have a heart-to-heart talk with her."

People who wear only ready-made clothes are apt to doubt the very existence of tailors; and this pair, enthralled though they were by ready-made tragedies, had no way of knowing that there were people who had their tragedies made to order. Etsuko was, as ever, written in an alphabet they couldn't read.

* * * *

The rain started in the morning of October eleventh. They had to close the storm shutters because of the wind and rain. To make matters worse, they had no electric power in the daytime. The downstairs rooms, dark as a root cellar, echoed depressingly with the crying of Natsuo and the pertinaciously chorusing voice of his sister. Nobuko had stayed home from school—out of sorts because she hadn't been taken to the festival.

These annoyances drove Yakichi and Etsuko to pay a

rare visit to Kensuke's quarters. The second floor was not equipped with storm shutters, for the windows were fitted strongly with glass. No rain blew in, but in one place a leak had developed. A bucket lined with cloths stood under it.

This was an epoch-making visit. Yakichi, who preferred to keep to himself, and had built for himself a restricted area within his own home, had never visited Kensuke's or Asako's rooms. As a result, on seeing his father enter, Kensuke spared no effort to show Yakichi how honored he was and ran about helping Chieko prepare tea. Yakichi was appropriately impressed.

"Don't go to any trouble. We're just seeking refuge."

"Please don't bother yourselves."

As they spoke, Yakichi and Etsuko seemed to fall into the pose of children playing office, acting the parts of the boss and his wife visiting the home of a subordinate.

"I couldn't tell what Etsuko was thinking the way she was sitting, hidden just a little behind Father," Chieko said later.

The rain encompassed everything in a tight, dense wall. The wind had abated somewhat, but the sound of the downpour was still overpowering. Etsuko turned to watch the rain water coursing like India ink down the jet-black trunk of a persimmon tree. She felt here as if she were shut up in the sound of merciless, monotonous, oppressive music . . .

The sound of the rain is like the voices of tens of thousands of monks reading sutras. Yakichi is chattering, Kensuke is chattering, Chieko is chattering—how useless words are! What petty craft, what futility! What diddling, bustling, everlasting-stretching-with-all-one's-might-for-something, meaningless activity!

No one's words can compete with this mercilessly powerful rain. The only thing that can compete with the sound of this rain, that can smash this deathlike wall of sound, is the shout of a man who refuses to stoop to this chatter, the shout of a simple spirit that knows no words. Etsuko recalled the mass of rose-color naked figures running before her in the light of the flaming poles, and the sound of their shouting, like the cries of slippery young animals.

Only that shout! That's all that's needed!

Etsuko suddenly came back to the moment. Yakichi's voice had elevated in pitch. Her opinion was being demanded.

"What will we do about Miyo? If her partner in this thing is Saburo, he is the one who must decide. We'll have to go by what he thinks right. If he insists on dodging his responsibility, we won't keep the irresponsible cur in the house. We'll fire him and keep only Miyo. Then we'll arrange an abortion for her child, and that will be that.

"If, though, Saburo honestly owns up to his guilt, he can marry Miyo. They'll be man and wife, and all will be as it should be.

"Those are our two alternatives. What do you think about them? My ideas are pretty radical, but that's because I'm trying to go by the spirit of the new constitution."

Etsuko did not reply. She uttered a faint, perhaps inaudible "Well . . ." and focused her exquisite black eyes on a random spot somewhere in the sky. The noise of the rain somehow justified her silence. Kensuke looked at her and fancied she had a streak of madness in her.

"You don't seem to be able to figure out how we should proceed, do you, Etsuko?" said Kensuke, helpfully.

Yakichi, however, did not waver. He had no intention of

being patient. He was proposing these alternatives in the presence of Kensuke and his wife because he felt a burning need to test Etsuko. His question was contrived to force her either to defend Saburo by recommending the marriage or, in order that she might allay the suspicions of the others, to revile Saburo—however much it went against her grain—and join in the plan to get rid of him. If Yakichi's old friends had seen him stoop to such mild measures as this, they would have doubted their eyes.

Yakichi's jealousy was inexpressibly degrading. If, in the prime of his life, he had seen his wife captivated by another man, he probably would have wiped those strange ideas out of her head with a single swipe of the rough back of his hand. Fortunately, his dead wife was never thus afflicted. She was a woman resolutely pursuing the charming irrelevance of educating him in the ways of high society. Now Yakichi was old. His was an aging process that worked from the inside out—an aging process like that which might attack a stuffed eagle, its insides hollowed by white ants. With Etsuko's stealthy attachment for Saburo developing under his eyes, Yakichi took no decisive step.

Etsuko looked at the jealousy flashing in this old man's eyes in all its powerlessness and degradation and thought of the potency of her own jealousy, of the thing that filled her with its inexhaustible store, of the "ability to suffer" of which she was constantly aware and was tempted to boast of to any who would hear.

Etsuko answered to the point, joyfully and to the point. "I intend to speak to Saburo and ask him for the truth. I think this is a better course than your talking to him directly, Father."

One common danger allied Etsuko and Yakichi. It was not the mutual benefit that makes allies of the ordinary nations of this world; it was jealousy.

After that the four talked agreeably until noon. When they returned to their rooms, Yakichi sent Etsuko back to Kensuke's quarters with a whole pint of their fine Shiba chestnuts.

While preparing lunch, Etsuko burned one of her fingers slightly and broke a small dish.

When the food was soft, Yakichi had nothing but fine things to say about it. When it was hard he found it tasteless. He judged Etsuko's cooking not by how it tasted, but by how soft it was.

On rainy days, when the veranda was closed off, Etsuko cooked in the kitchen. The rice Miyo had cooked the day before had not been transferred to a tub but had been kept in the pot in order to retain the warm taste. Only the rice remained as evidence that she had been there. The charcoal embers showed no sign of life. Etsuko went to Chieko for hot coals with which to start a fire; while she was transferring them to the clay stove, she burned her middle finger.

The pain annoyed Etsuko. What if she screamed? Under no circumstances would it be Saburo who would hear her scream and come running. It would be Yakichi who would bustle in, his ugly, brown, wrinkled legs showing out of his open robe, and would say: "What's wrong?" It would never be Saburo.

She felt like laughing—a loud, mad laugh. Again, though, there would be Yakichi. His eyes would narrow. He wouldn't laugh with her; he would simply strive to figure out the reason for her laughter. He was not of an age to join voices and laugh unreservedly with a woman. Yet he was her only echo, her only reverberation; and she was a woman none would call old.

A puddle of rainwater covered part of the twenty square yards or so of the kitchen's earthen floor, reflecting the gray light coming lazily through the glass door. Etsuko stood barefoot in her damp, sticky *geta,* held her burned finger against the tip of her tongue and absentmindedly looked toward the door. Her head was full of the sound of rain.

Assuredly, daily life is a ridiculous thing. Her hands began to move as if they were no longer tied. She put the pot on the fire. She poured water. She poured sugar. She cut sweet potatoes into round slices and put them in it. The menu for today's lunch would be candied sweet potato, ground beef she had purchased at Okamachi with sautéed *hatsutaké* mushrooms, and grated yam—all put together by her absentminded energies. All the while she wandered about, dreaming like a scullery maid.

But the pain hasn't started yet. Why not? I'm not yet really suffering. Pain should turn my heart to ice, make my hands shake, tie up my legs. Who is this me, here preparing a meal? Why am I doing this?

Cool judgment, accurate judgment, judgment seasoned with sentiment—these things I can still use and shall continue to use far into the future. But Miyo's pregnancy should have made my misery complete! Something must be missing. It must be that something more terrible must be added to that completeness.

First I must follow through with the plan I have contrived so carefully. It will be painful to see Saburo; it certainly won't be fun. But married! To me? (I must be out of my mind.) To Miyo! To that country wench, that rotten tomato, that stupid girl smelling of urine!

Thus my suffering will be complete. My suffering will be a perfect thing, a finished thing. Then maybe I will get some relief. A brief, a false ease will be mine. That I shall cling to. That chimera I shall trust . . .

Etsuko heard the chirping of a chickadee by the window frame. She pressed her forehead to the glass and watched the little bird adjusting the feathers of its wet wings. A thin white patch that looked like an eyelid kept winking down across the bird's tiny, flashing black eye. At its throat a fine break in the feathers kept moving; from there the peevish chirping came.

She saw something very bright in the distance. The rain had now slowed to a drizzle. The center of the chestnut grove at the edge of the garden was growing bright, opening like a gold niche in a dark temple.

In the afternoon the rain cleared away.

Etsuko went out into the garden with Yakichi to repair the roses that had lost their supports in the storm. Some roses were floating face-down in the muddy, grass-strewn rainwater. Mutilated petals drifted beside them.

Etsuko rescued one flower and tied it to a righted support with a piece of string. Fortunately the stem had not broken. Her fingers felt the weight of the petals of which Yakichi was so proud. As she touched each flower Etsuko looked deep into the marvelous, scarlet petals from which the fresh, clinging sensation came.

Yakichi, however, was out of sorts as he worked at this task—expressionless, silent in his rubber boots, his army trousers tight on his legs as he stooped to pick up the roses. This uncommunicative, expressionless toil was the toil of a man whose blood still bespoke his farmer's lineage. Even Etsuko was attracted to the Yakichi of times like this.

Then Saburo came down the gravel path before Etsuko's eyes and called to them: "Excuse me. I didn't know you were out here. I'll get ready and do that for you."

"We've finished. It's all right," said Yakichi, without looking at Saburo.

Saburo's light brown face smiled at Etsuko from under his great straw hat. The battered brim of the hat was pulled down at an angle. The western sun etched a bright streak across his forehead. The stark whiteness of the teeth in his smiling mouth—the fresh whiteness of them, as if washed by rain—made Etsuko's eyes open wider as she stood up.

"Just on time. I want to talk to you. Would you walk with me over that way?"

Etsuko had never before spoken to Saburo in such friendly tones in the presence of Yakichi. Her words suggested a free and easy association unmindful of Yakichi; one who heard these phrases alone could have taken them as boldly inviting. She had closed her eyes to the cruel duty she had to perform later and had uttered her words half drunk with the joy of them. As a result, an unanticipated, unrestrained sweetness floated about what she said.

Saburo looked doubtfully toward Yakichi. Etsuko, however, already had him by the elbow and was propelling him down the path in the direction of the entrance to the Sugimoto home.

"Are you just going to walk around and talk it over?" Yakichi called after them, in a somewhat flustered voice.

"Yes," said Etsuko. Her quick reactions—impulsive, almost unconscious—had deprived Yakichi of the opportunity of being present at her confrontation with Saburo.

Her first words to Saburo were rather meaningless: "Where were you going just now?"

"I was going to mail a letter."

"A letter? Let me see."

Saburo politely displayed a postcard he had been holding rolled up in his hand. It was a reply to a letter he had received from a friend at home. The writing was quite childish; it set forth Saburo's most recent history in only four or five simple lines: "Yesterday we had the festival here. I went out with the Young Men's League and made a lot of noise. I'm really beat today. It was all very exciting, though, and fun."

Etsuko's shoulders shook as she laughed.

"It's to the point," she said, returning the card to Saburo. He seemed a little dissatisfied by her comment.

The gravel path through the *kaede* trees was splashed everywhere with spots of sun and drops of rain slipping through the leaves. On some trees the leaves were already red; their branches turned in the wind. As Etsuko and Saburo reached the stairs, the sky that had until then been hidden by foliage suddenly opened out. They were aware for the first time of the all-enveloping mackerel sky.

This joy beyond speech, this silent richness beyond

words, created in Etsuko a kind of guilt. Here was this tiny period of peace vouchsafed her in order to make her misery complete. She began to be astonished at the joy she had been taking in it. Was she going to go on forever with this absurd conversation and never get to the unpleasant issue?

They crossed the bridge. The creek had swelled; in the muddy torrent great masses of water plants streamed with the current—fresh, green tresses appearing and disappearing. They went through the bamboo grove and came to a path from which a fresh view of the rain-washed ricefields spread. Saburo stopped and took off his hat.

"Well, goodbye."

"Are you going to mail your card?"

"Yes."

"I want to talk to you. Would you mail it afterward?"

"Yes, ma'am."

In Saburo's eyes a tinge of anxiety showed. How could the ever-distant Etsuko deal with him here so intimately? This was the first time he had felt her and her words at such close range. He reached his hand to his back uneasily.

"Is something wrong with your back?" asked Etsuko.

"Yes, I got scraped a little in the festival last night."

"Does it hurt much?" she asked, bringing her brows together.

"No. It's better already," he said cheerfully.

His young flesh is indestructible, thought Etsuko.

The mud and the soaking-wet weeds along the path dirtied their feet. After a time the path narrowed; they could no longer walk side by side. Etsuko went ahead, lifting her skirts slightly. She suddenly began to wonder whether Saburo was following her. She was tempted to call his name but found it awkward either to call to him or turn to look at him.

"Was that a bicycle?" she asked, turning back toward him.

"No." His bewildered face was right by hers.

"Oh, I thought I heard a bell," she said, looking down. It pleased her to see his great, clumsy bare feet beside her bare feet, spotted with the same mud.

As usual, there were no automobiles on the highway. The untraveled concrete surface had dried quickly. Only a few puddles here and there reflected the mackerel sky. Its vivid line, looking as if it had been drawn with chalk, disappeared into the horizon and the pale blue evening sky.

"Have you heard that Miyo is pregnant?" Etsuko asked, walking beside him.

"Yes. I've heard it."

"From whom?"

"From Miyo."

"I see."

Etsuko felt her heartbeat quicken. She felt she had to hear the painful truth from Saburo's own lips. There was at the root of her resolve a complex hope which made her think that Saburo might have contrary evidence. For instance, that Miyo's lover was a certain Maidemmura youth, a notorious person whom Saburo had warned her about, though she had scorned his advice. Or, for instance, that she was involved with some married man among the union executives . . .

These possibilities and these impossibilities revolved in Etsuko's brain, each in its turn threatening her, each alternately standing for the truth, with the result that her heart kept putting off the fatal question. What seemed like a myriad of joyful particles hidden in the rain-fresh air, what seemed like a myriad of elements hurrying, dancing toward a new combining—all these pellucid intimations struck their nostrils and made their cheeks glow as they walked in silence for a time on the untraveled road.

"Now Miyo's child—" Etsuko said, suddenly. "Now Miyo's child—who is its father?"

Saburo did not answer. Etsuko waited. Still he did not answer. When silence is prolonged over a certain period of time, it takes on new meaning. Etsuko could not bear to wait until that period had elapsed. She closed her eyes. Then she opened them again. It seemed as if she were the one being pressed for an answer. She looked stealthily at the silhouette of Saburo's stubbornly down-turned profile beneath his straw hat.

"Is it yours?"

"I guess so."

"You guess so? And perhaps you guess not?"

"No." Saburo's face reddened. He forced a smile, though not very far: "It's mine."

It had been too quick—Etsuko chewed her lip in consternation. She had taken refuge in the faint hope that he would divine that common courtesy to her called for a denial, even a clumsy, outright lie. But now that hope was gone. If she held any part of his heart, surely he would not have made the admission he had just made. This truth that Yakichi and Kensuke had arrived at, and which she herself had already grasped as self-evident—the truth that Saburo was the child's father—she had been convinced that Saburo would in the end, out of fear and embarrassment, deny.

"Well," Etsuko said, as if she were tired. There was no power in her words: "Then you love Miyo?"

Here was a word that meant nothing to Saburo. It was out of his ken, part of the lexicon of luxury, of articles made to order. It was somehow superfluous, devoid of urgency, forced. In the urgent but not at all lasting relationship that bound him and Miyo—like that of two compasses drawn to each other through force when within a certain radius of each other but not drawn at all when outside that radius—the word *love* had no proper place.

He had expected that Yakichi would make them separate, which would have caused him little pain. Even after he had been informed of Miyo's pregnancy, the consciousness that he was a father had still not been born in this young gardener.

In response to Etsuko's interrogations, various recollections formed in his mind. One day, about a month after Etsuko had come to Maidemmura, Yakichi had sent Miyo to the shed for a shovel, which was wedged deep inside the shed so that she could not pull it out. She had gone to Saburo for help, and he pulled it out for her.

There she was while he strained at the shovel, her head just under his arms, perhaps to cheer him on, while she held back an old table that was lying against the shovel. Saburo could smell the strong odor of the cream she used on her face mixed with the moldy smells of the shed. He held the freed shovel out to Miyo, but she didn't take it. Instead she stood there wordlessly staring up at him. Saburo's arms reached out unconsciously and embraced her.

Was that love?

When the spring rains were almost over, and the hot chafing pressures of the last part of this captive season nagged at him, Saburo suddenly decided to slip out of his window into the night rain. He made a half circle around the house and tapped at Miyo's window. Through the glass he could see Miyo's face clear and white as she slept.

She opened her eyes and saw Saburo's face peering from the shadows outside the window and then the white line of his teeth. With what strange swiftness this girl who did everything so slowly during the day now threw aside her bed clothes and jumped up! Her nightgown was loose at the neck; one breast was exposed. It was a tense, straining breast, like a bent bow, enough to make one believe that it was what had thrown the nightgown from her bosom.

Miyo opened the window, taking extreme care that she made no noise. Saburo stood before her, wordlessly pointing to his muddy feet. She ran for a rag, had him sit on the window frame, and then carefully wiped his feet clean.

Was that love?

This chain of associations passed through Saburo's mind in an instant. He desired her, he was sure; but he did not love her. All day, every day, his thoughts turned only to when the weeding had to be done, to how, if war broke out again, he would fulfill his dreams of peril by enlisting in the navy, to reveries about the prophecies of Tenri and their fulfillment, to the day when the world would end and the manna would fall from heaven on Tenri's manna table, to his happy grade-school days and romps through mountain and meadow, to what he would have for supper. He didn't think about Miyo so much as one one hundredth of the day.

He desired her—even that notion seemed less tenable the more he thought about it. It was like a yearning for food. Any internal struggle to vanquish his desires was of no concern to this healthy young man.

Thus Saburo reflected for a moment on this incomprehensible question and then shook his head as if puzzled: "No."

Etsuko could not believe her ears.

Joy flashed from her face like agony. Saburo did not see her expression; his eyes were caught by the Hankyu train that sped barely visible behind the trees. If he had seen that expression he would have been taken aback by the pain his answer seemed to cause Etsuko. Surely he would have changed it.

"If you don't love her . . ." Etsuko spoke slowly, sucking the joy out of each word. "Was that your honest . . ." She seemed to be trying to induce Saburo to say that "No" again without running the risk of having him say the opposite. "It doesn't matter whether you love her or not, so long as you say exactly what you feel. You don't love Miyo, do you?"

Saburo barely heeded her repetition of these words. " 'Love her . . . don't love her'—what a meaningless waste of time," he thought. "She's mouthing over this stupid matter as if it were enough to turn the world upside-down." He thrust his fingers deep in his pockets and came upon some pieces of the dried cuttlefish he had eaten with his *saké* at the festival the night before.

"What if I start munching on a piece of this cuttlefish? I wonder what kind of face she'll make," he said to himself.

Etsuko's seriousness made him wish to tease her. He took a piece of the cuttlefish out of his pocket, gleefully flipped it with his fingers, and caught it in his mouth as would a frolicking dog. Then he said, unabashed: "That's right. I don't love her."

It wouldn't have made any difference if this busybody of

an Etsuko had gone to Miyo and reported to her: "Saburo said he doesn't love you." These impulsive lovers had never taken the trouble to discuss whether they loved each other or not.

Prolonged suffering makes one stupid; but one made stupid by suffering knows joy when he sees it. It was from this standpoint that Etsuko watched, calculating all. She did not realize that she was a convert to Yakichi's self-made code of justice. Saburo did not love Miyo; therefore he had to marry her. To make matters worse, she hid behind the mask of the hypocrite and took joy in goading Saburo by the moral judgment that says: "A man who fathers a child on a woman he doesn't love must take the responsibility of marrying her."

"You're an awful rascal," said Etsuko. "You don't love her, but you made her pregnant; and now you have to marry Miyo."

Saburo suddenly turned his sharp, beautiful eyes toward Etsuko and returned her gaze. Her voice became harder; it helped her to repel that look: "Don't say you don't want to. The Sugimoto family has always understood its young people, but it has never tolerated irresponsibility. Father has ordered that you two get married, and you'll do just that."

Saburo was shocked; he had not expected this. He had believed that, at worst, Yakichi would insist they have nothing more to do with each other. If, though, marriage was what he wanted, all well and good. The only consideration left was what his fault-finding mother would say.

"I'd better find out what my mother thinks."

"And how do you feel?" Etsuko would not be content until she had personally persuaded Saburo into the marriage.

"If the master says I should marry Miyo, I'll marry her," he said. After all, it was not a matter of very great moment.

"It will be a load off my shoulders," said Etsuko, cheerfully. It certainly did simplify matters.

She was beguiled by her own projections, intoxicated by the happy, happy situation of Saburo married to Miyo *against his will.* Was her intoxication like that of the woman who has assuaged her heart's pangs with wine? Was it wine drunk not so much to gain inebriation as oblivion, not so much to induce visions as blindness—in short, to arrive deliberately at stupid judgments? Was not this overwhelming drunkenness part of her unconscious plan to avoid injury to herself?

The word marriage was absolutely terrifying to Etsuko, and she now wished to turn over the handling of this ominous term to Yakichi. It was his responsibility, conferred by his arbitrary ruling. In this respect she was dependent upon Yakichi, and she stared over his shoulder like a child on its parent's back beholding some terrifying sight.

At the point where the road past the Okamachi station swung right to merge with the highway, they encountered two large, beautiful cars coming onto the concrete surface. One was pearly white; the other was a new, pale-blue Chevrolet. Motors purring soft as velvet, they curved past. The first vehicle was filled with laughing young men and women. As it moved past Etsuko, she could hear the sound of jazz music from the radio. The second car had a Japanese chauffeur. In the dim recesses of its back seat, a sharp-eyed couple—blond hair darkening into age—sat motionless, like birds of prey.

Saburo's mouth opened slightly; he gazed at them in wonder.

"They're going back to Osaka, aren't they?" said Etsuko. As she spoke, suddenly the noise of all the turmoil of the city seemed to float to her on the wind and strike her ears.

To Etsuko, who knew how little was to be found by one who went off there, the city held none of the attractions it held for country folk. To be sure, the city was like a building that offered visions of ever-new mystery, but for Etsuko that soaring structure held no charm.

Etsuko burned with desire to have Saburo take her arm in his. Leaning on that arm, bordered with golden hair, she would walk down this road anywhere. Before long they would be in Osaka, in the very center of all that metropolitan congestion. Before long they would be washed forward by waves of humanity. She would wake suddenly and look around her in amazement. From that moment, it seemed, Etsuko's *real life* would begin.

Would Saburo take her arm?

This stolid youth was bored by this widow older than he walking silently beside him. He was completely unconscious of her hair done up morning after morning with such care for him alone. Only curiosity led him to glance at the mysterious plaits of her splendid, fragrant coiffure. He would not have dreamed that inside this strangely distant, strangely haughty woman spun the girlish fancy that he might lock her arm in his. He stopped suddenly and did an about-face.

"Must we go back already?" asked Etsuko. Her eyes pleaded with him, brimming eyes tinged faintly with blue, as if reflecting the evening sky.

"It's late, madam . . ."

They had come further than they realized. Far off above the shadowy forest the roofs of the Sugimoto home gleamed in the setting sun.

It took them a half hour to walk back there.

* * * *

Then Etsuko's real misery began—that misery arranged so carefully in all its details. It was the misery of the unlucky man who has worked all his life to accomplish a task at last successful, who as soon as it is done must face death, suffer, and die. Those watching might not be able to decide whether he had striven all his days to complete the task or to gain the privilege of suffering and dying in his splendid, private hospital suite.

Etsuko had planned to wait patiently, joyfully, over any period of time, for Miyo's unhappiness, for Miyo's misery to grow like mold and batten on her. She would wait unfalteringly, eyes never swerving, as this loveless marriage developed and fell into the same wreckage Etsuko's had fallen into some time before. She would give her life to see it with her own eyes. She would wait until her hair turned white if she had to. She did not insist that she be Saburo's mistress. All that was necessary was that Miyo, before Etsuko's eyes, should lose hope, should fall into agony, into distraction, into exhaustion, into collapse.

Beyond a shadow of a doubt, however, that calculation had failed.

In accordance with Etsuko's advice, Yakichi made public the relationship of Miyo and Saburo. To the queries of the backbiting villagers, he proclaimed: "They're getting married."

To maintain the order of the house, he had them remain in the same distantly separate rooms as before. Once a week, though, they were allowed to sleep in the same room. Saburo was waiting for the October twenty-sixth Tenri Fall Festival, and after he spoke to his mother there, arrangements for the marriage—with Yakichi to serve as matchmaker—would be completed.

Yakichi managed matters with a kind of passion. With a kindly old gaffer's smile he had never worn before alight on his face, with a demeanor of all too perfect understanding, he grandiloquently tolerated the courtship of Saburo and Miyo. Needless to say, the thought of Etsuko was ever present in this, Yakichi's new attitude.

What a fortnight that was! Etsuko relived with renewed force the sleepless nights of those tortured days of late summer stretching into autumn when her husband never came home. In the daytime how the time had dragged, how she had vacillated over whether she should or should not phone him, how every approaching footstep had caused her anguish! For days she had not been able to swallow food; she merely drank water and lay in bed. One morning when she took a drink of water and felt its coolness spread in her body, she suddenly thought of poisoning herself. As she imagined the joy of feeling the white crystals of the poison spread in the water and quietly penetrate her system, Etsuko fell into a kind of rapture and shed tears that caused her not the slightest pain.

She felt again the symptoms of that time—the unexplainable cold shivers, the paroxysms that brought gooseflesh even to the palms of her hands. Surely this was the cold of prison. Surely captive men shivered like this.

Just as once the absence of Ryosuke had tortured her,

now the very sight of Saburo brought her pain. When, that spring, he had gone to Tenri, she had felt closer to him than when he had been nearby. But now her hands were tied. She had to sit by and watch him and Miyo indulge in all their intimacies and not raise a finger. Hers was a cruel, heartless punishment. Moreover, it was a punishment imposed by herself.

She hated herself for not having advised Yakichi to discharge Saburo and abort Miyo's baby. Her regret was so deep that it cut the ground from under her. Out of her natural desire not to be separated from Saburo, she had brought upon herself this terrible agony.

Was there not, however, an element of self-deception in Etsuko's remorse? Did she not realize this pain would reverse itself against her? Was it not a natural pain—one she might have anticipated, willed, in fact, coveted? Had not Etsuko herself, not very long before, fervently wished to bring upon herself the supreme pain?

On October fifteenth the fruit market was to open in Okamachi. Since the choicest produce would be sent to Osaka, the clear skies of October thirteenth seemed made to order. The Sugimoto family, along with the Okura family, therefore put all their effort into harvesting the persimmons, which were the finest of the fruits this year.

Saburo climbed the trees, and Miyo waited beneath him, keeping him supplied with empty baskets. The branches swung back and forth, making the blue sky, visible in patches through the branches, seem to reel and totter. Miyo watched Saburo's feet as he moved about among the leaves.

"It's full!" Saburo called. The basket full of shining persimmons struck the lowest branches and was received in Miyo's upstretched hands. She lowered it impassively to the ground. She stood with her legs wide apart in their cotton pantaloons as she untied the basket and sent up an empty one.

"Come up here," said Saburo.

"Coming," she answered, and climbed the tree with surprising swiftness.

Etsuko heard voices in the tree. She was wearing a cloth over her hair, and her sleeves were tied back with a cord as she approached with a pile of empty baskets. She could see Saburo defending himself against Miyo. He was trying to pry her hands loose from the branch she was holding to; she was screaming and reaching for his ankle, which hung down in front of her. They could not see Etsuko, since she was concealed by the branches.

Now Miyo bit Saburo's fingers. He laughed and cursed at her. She climbed to a branch above that which he occupied and threatened to kick him in the face. He grabbed her knee and held it. Until this time the branches had moved in great swings. Now the branches gaily festooned with leaves and persimmons—still plentiful—tossed as if moved by gentle breezes. The branches nearby shook in concert.

Etsuko closed her eyes and moved away. Something like ice ran down her spine.

Maggie barked.

Kensuke was sitting on a mat outside the kitchen door, along with Mrs. Okura and Asako, sorting persimmons. It never took him long to find the job that took the least work.

"Etsuko? Where are the persimmons?" he called. She did not answer.

"What's wrong? You're as white as a sheet," he said. Etsuko said nothing. She passed through the kitchen and out the other door and walked unconsciously to the shade of the pasanias. There she threw the empty baskets to the ground, slumped to her knees and covered her face with her hands.

That evening at supper, Yakichi put down his chopsticks and said cheerfully: "Saburo and Miyo are like a pair of puppy dogs. Miyo was making a fuss today about an ant crawling down her back. I was there, but figured it was Saburo's job to get it off her. He went over to her looking as if it was all a great bother—like a monkey that doesn't know any tricks.

"But somehow he couldn't find the ant, no matter how much he felt around. It was hard to tell whether it had really been there in the first place. Pretty soon, though, Miyo began to get ticklish and started laughing, laughing and squirming about as if she'd die. Have you ever heard of someone having a miscarriage because she'd laughed too much? According to Kensuke, the child of a woman who laughs a lot grows fast after he is born because he gets massaged so well in his mother's womb."

This tale, combined with what she had seen earlier that day, made Etsuko feel as if every inch of her body had been impaled with needles. Her neck felt as if clamped in a pillory of ice. Spiritual pain was slowly taking possession of her body, soaking into it as a flooding river soaks the ricefields. Her spirit seemed tired of its role; it seemed to be sending out distress signals.

Are you all right? Your boat is about to go under. And haven't you even called for help yet? You have abused the ship of your spirit and deprived yourself of harbor. So now the time has come that you must swim the sea by your own power. All you have before you is death. Is that what you want?

Pain alone can thus serve as a warning. In its last extremity, her organism was apt to lose its spiritual support. Her despair was like a headache pounding to the bursting point, a great glass ball sliding up into her throat from deep inside her.

I'll never call for help, she thought.

In spite of everything, Etsuko needed the wild logic that would help her to build a foundation on which she could call herself happy.

I must swallow it, no matter what . . . I must affirm—with eyes closed—no matter what . . . This pain I must learn to savor . . . One who pans for gold can't expect to dip up only gold, or even attempt to. He must blindly scoop the sand from the river bottom. He doesn't have the privilege of finding out in advance whether he will succeed. Maybe there's no gold in it, but maybe there is. Yet the one thing certain is that the person who doesn't pan for gold never gets any richer.

Her thoughts went on: *a surer way to happiness is to drink up the water that flows into the ocean from the rivers. That's what I've been doing up to this time. I suppose that's what I'll continue doing. My stomach can stand it.*

Thus the infinitude of pain leads one to believe in the indestructibility of the body by pain. And is that, after all, so silly?

• • •

The day before the market opened, Okura and Saburo took a shipment to the market place. After they had left, Yakichi swept up the scraps of twine, of paper, of straw, of fallen leaves and broken bamboo baskets, and started a fire. He had Etsuko watch the fire while he swept up what was left of the litter.

The afternoon was darkened by fog. One could not distinguish between the fog and the approaching darkness. Evening seemed to be coming on earlier than usual. The moody, smoky sunset exuded a strangely attenuated gleam; a faint drop of afterglow lit the gray, blotting-paper surface of the fog.

For some reason or other Yakichi felt uneasy about leaving Etsuko alone there, even for a moment. Perhaps it was the shadowy look of her in the fog at a distance of just a few yards. The color of the fire was breathtakingly beautiful in the mist. Etsuko was standing still, staring into the fire, and occasionally raking up scattered straw with a bamboo rake. The fire seemed to leap toward her hands as if enticing them.

Yakichi circled about Etsuko idly and left his sweepings beside her. Then he circled off again. When he came close he would look furtively at Etsuko's face. She paused in her mechanical movement of the rake and, though she could not have been cold, held her hand up to a particularly high burst of flame emanating from one of the broken baskets that were constantly, noisily flaring up.

"Etsuko!" Yakichi shouted, throwing down his broom and running to pull her away from the fire. She had burned the palm of her hand in the flames.

This burn was beyond comparison with that she had suffered on her middle finger a while ago. Her right hand was, for the time being, useless. The soft skin of her palm was raised in one large blister. The pain of that hand, coated with salve and swathed in many layers of bandage, brought her little rest that night.

Yakichi recalled with terror how she had looked at that instant. Where did she get the composure with which she looked so fearlesly into the fire, with which she extended her hands to the flames—that firm, plastic composure? It was an almost arrogant *sang-froid*. This woman given over to confused tides of feeling had for a moment broken free from those tides.

If she had been left alone, perhaps she would not have been burned. Yakichi's voice had awakened her from that state of equilibrium that is possible only in the doze of the spirit, and then, it seemed, her hand was burned for the first time.

* * * *

Yakichi was frightened simply by looking at Etsuko's bandage. He seemed to feel that he himself had inflicted the burn. The wound was not a small thing with this woman one could never call careless, this woman whose customary composure was enough to make others uncomfortable. When, a few days before, she had worn the small bandage on her finger and Yakichi had asked her about it, she had answered simply that her finger was burned. Surely she had not burned it herself. With that bandage barely off she had now acquired a broad bandage covering her whole hand.

When Yakichi was young he told his friends that a

woman's health was made up of many illnesses. He was proud of that dictum, which he had arrived at by himself. One of his friends, for instance, had married a woman troubled by mysterious stomach pains. Soon after they were married her pains went away. Then, however, as their marriage dulled, she fell prey to recurrent migraine headaches. Her husband was exceedingly annoyed by them and began to turn to other women for solace. When his wife realized this her migraine disappeared. Then, however, her premarital stomach pains returned, and after a year she died of stomach cancer. One can never tell how much of a woman's illness is lie and how much truth. When you think it's a lie, suddenly she has a child or dies.

"A woman's accidents are another thing," thought Yakichi. "My friend Karajima was a great friend of the ladies. When he started to run around, his wife started accidentally breaking plates—one a day. It was pure accident; for his wife, it seemed, wasn't really conscious that he was unfaithful. She was innocently amazed each day by the blunders unconsciously committed by her fingertips."

Then one day Yakichi himself did something quite unusual; he ran a thorn into his finger while sweeping the garden. He left it alone, and the finger became slightly infected. But then the pus came out all by itself, and it healed perfectly. Yakichi didn't like medicine, and never used it.

During the day he saw Etsuko's distress at close range. At night he was aware of her restlessness beside him and caressed her more importunately for it. Naturally he was jealous of Saburo, and Etsuko was jealous of Miyo. He was also jealous of Etsuko's unrequited love. Yet there was in his jealous heart a hint of gratefulness for the stimulation jealousy gave his love-making.

Thus he would exaggerate stories about Saburo and Miyo just to torture Etsuko, and at such times felt a certain affinity, in fact an affection, for them. Out of fear of losing her, however, he didn't indulge in this sport too often. She had become something he could not do without—a necessity, like a sin or a bad habit.

Etsuko was a beautiful eczema. At Yakichi's age he couldn't itch without eczema.

Yet if Yakichi became a little more considerate and moderated his tales about Saburo and Miyo, Etsuko became strangely uneasy. She wondered if some new development had occurred that he did not want her to know about. Could there be any development worse than this? Such a question might have been asked by one who had never been jealous. Jealousy does not, after all, have to feed on factual evidence; in that respect its passions are close to the passions of idealism.

They bathed once a week, and Yakichi went in first. Usually Etsuko bathed with him, but this evening she felt a cold coming on, and he went in alone.

All the women of the Sugimoto family were in the kitchen. Etsuko, Chieko, Asako, Miyo, even Nobuko were washing their various dishes at the same time. Etsuko was wearing a white silk cloth around her neck because of her cold.

Asako mentioned her husband in Siberia: "I haven't received a letter from him since August. He's a terrible correspondent, I know, but I would think he could write at least once a week. Naturally, the love of a man and wife can't be expressed only in words, but the great fault of Japanese men is their laziness about using words and phrases to express matters of the heart."

Chieko was amused to think how Yusuke, perhaps burrowing under the tundra with the temperature far below zero, would react if he heard these words.

"Yes, but if he did write once a week they wouldn't send that many letters. For all we know, he may be writing that often."

"If so I wonder where all those letters are going."

"They must be giving them to Russian widows, surely."

After she said this, Chieko realized that her words might have offended Etsuko, but Asako's reply, which showed that she did not see the joke, saved the day: "Maybe so, but surely they can't read Japanese."

Chieko dropped out of the conversation and turned to help Etsuko with her dishes: "Let me wash them; you'll get your bandage wet."

"Thank you."

In reality Etsuko did not wish to be relieved of the mechanical chore of washing cups and dishes. Lately she longed with an almost sensual desire to turn herself into a machine. She looked forward to the time when her hand healed and with great speed she would sew fall kimonos for herself and Yakichi. The cloth for them had already been washed and seamed. Her needle would fly with superhuman speed.

The kitchen was lighted by only a naked twenty-watt bulb, which hung down between the smoky beams of the ceiling. There at the sink dark with their shadows the women had to do their washing. Etsuko leaned against the window frame and watched Miyo closely as she washed the pots. Beneath her shoddy, faded muslin sash, the flesh of her hips swelled faintly.

She looks as if she's going to lay an egg right now. Robust girl that she is, she's not troubled by morning sickness. In the summer she wears loose, short-sleeved, one-piece dresses, but she doesn't even know enough to shave her armpits. When she sweats a lot, she takes a towel, no matter who is around, and wipes her armpits.

The ripeness of her hips—like fruit. Those curves like coiled springs that once Etsuko too had possessed. That expansiveness, like a heavy, massive flower vase brimming with water.

And Saburo did all that. That young gardener planted his seeds ever so carefully, cultivated them with such solicitude. Just as in the morning the petals of the tiger lily wet with dew cling together as if they'll never part, her nipples and his breast had clung together wet with sweat.

Suddenly Etsuko became conscious of Yakichi, talking loudly in the bathroom, adjacent to the kitchen. Saburo was outside keeping the water heater supplied with wood. Yakichi was speaking to him.

The overexuberant way he splashed the bath water called up the image of his aging, cadaverous body, its collarbones filled with tiny pools of water. She could hear his cracked voice bouncing from the ceiling as he called: "Saburo! Saburo!"

"Yes, sir."

"Be careful about the firewood. Beginning today you

and Miyo bathe at the same time, and don't stay in long. If you bathe one at a time, you take too long and use at least a log or two more than necessary."

After Yakichi had bathed, Kensuke and Chieko went in. Then came Asako and her children. As they came out, Yakichi was surprised to hear Etsuko say she was going to take a quick bath.

Etsuko slipped into the tub and felt for the stopper with her toes. Only Saburo and Miyo had not yet bathed. She sank in the water up to her chin, reached down, and pulled the plug.

The reason for her action was not very deep: *Saburo and Miyo won't bathe together if I have anything to do with it.* For this insignificant reason, Etsuko had dared to take a bath in spite of her cold.

Yakichi had indulged himself by installing a bathroom four mats in area, with a square tub and slatted floor all of *hinoki* wood. The tub was wide and shallow, and down its drain, now with the plug pulled, the hot water sucked with a sound like the inward rushing of small shells. Etsuko smiled a smile of childish satisfaction that surprised even herself as she gazed into the dark, slightly dirty water.

What in the world am I doing? What's so exciting about this mischief? Even children have a serious reason for their mischief: to call the attention of the inattentive adult world to themselves. Mischief is the only recourse of the world of children. Yet rejected women feel the same rejection children do. They occupy the same rejected world, in which they grow cruel despite themselves.

• • •

On the surface of the water tiny hairs, oily micalike soap residue, and wood chips spun in slow circles. Etsuko rested her arm on the edge of the tub and then pressed her cheek within the curve of her bare shoulder. Water suddenly appeared on her shoulder and arm. Richly warm from the bath, her skin shone with a subdued gloss under the dim light bulb.

Etsuko's cheeks suddenly sensed the futility of the two shining, elastic arms pressed against them, sensed the humiliation, the sterility they shared. *It's no use! No use! No use!* she said to herself. The youth, the redundancy of this warm flesh—this blind, stupid animal—irritated her.

Her hair was piled high and held up with a comb. Drops of water fell occasionally from the ceiling on her hair and the nape of her neck, but she did nothing to avoid them, cold as they were. Into the bandage on her hand, held outside the tub, the cold drops soaked and disappeared.

The water slowly, ever so slowly, flowed down the drain. The line of the hot water and the air above it licked lazily down from her shoulder to her breast, from her breast to her stomach—delicate caresses that were soon gone, leaving her skin taut, her body swaddled in cold. Her back felt like ice. The water spun with a more rapid sound as it retreated from her hips and swirled down.

This is what death is. This is death.

Etsuko was about to scream for help when she came to herself. She was kneeling naked in the empty tub. Frightened, she rose.

On the way back to Yakichi's room, Etsuko met Miyo in the hall. She said, in a cheerful, yet bantering tone:

"Oh, I forgot. You two haven't bathed yet, and I've let out the water. I'm sorry."

The words were spoken so rapidly Miyo did not understand. She simply stood rooted, watching Etsuko's bloodless lips quiver.

* * * *

That evening Etsuko's fever began, and it kept her in bed for several days. On the third day her temperature was close to normal. It was October twenty-fourth.

Her convalescence was marked by extreme fatigue, and she woke from her afternoon nap that day to find the night already well advanced. Beside her lay Yakichi, breathing as if asleep.

The wall clock struck eleven softly yet uneasily; Maggie barked in the distance—endless repetitions of nights long ago dismissed as hopeless. Etsuko was struck with unbearable terror and woke Yakichi. He raised his checkered kimono-clad shoulder from the bed clothes, clumsily took Etsuko's outstretched hand and emitted a bewildered sigh.

"Hold my hand; don't let it go," said Etsuko, staring at a strange knot that loomed dimly in the wood ceiling. She did not look at Yakichi. He did not look at her.

Yakichi grunted, then hawked the phlegm deep in his throat and lapsed into silence. Soon he reached under his pillow for a piece of tissue, into which he spat.

After a time Etsuko said: "Miyo is sleeping in Saburo's room tonight, isn't she?"

"Well—"

"Don't try to hide it. I know. I don't have to see them; but I know what they're up to."

"Tomorrow morning Saburo is going to Tenri. The festival is the day after tomorrow. After all, when he's going away, what can you say?"

"Yes, what can you say?" Etsuko withdrew her hand, pulled the quilt over her head and burst into sobs.

Yakichi was puzzled by the strange position he had been placed in. "Why am I not angry?" he thought. "What does this mean—that I have lost the ability to be angry? How is it that this woman's unhappiness has made Yakichi feel like a conspirator?" He started to address Etsuko in a husky, tender, deliberately drowsy tone (Before he could fool the woman with this bedtime story he had concocted, he had to fool himself—irresolute, hopeless, his thoughts as slippery a those of a jellyfish).

"This boring country life must be getting on your nerves and pestering you with things that are of no importance. Soon it will be one year since Ryosuke died. I've promised you this before, but let's go to Tokyo, to the cemetery. I had Mr. Kamisaka sell some Kinki Railroad stock for me, and if we want to live it up, we can even go second-class. But if we save money on travel we'll have more to spend enjoying ourselves in Tokyo. We can go to plays, which neither of us has done for a long time. In Tokyo we'll never be without enjoyment of some kind.

"But the hope I have is much bigger than this. I'd like to leave Maidemmura and move to Tokyo. I'd even like to get back in harness. Two or three of my old friends in Tokyo have done it. They're not ungrateful ones like Miyahara; they're all men you can trust. So when we go to Tokyo I'll talk to two or three of them.

"That's what I'd like to do. It's not easy, but I'd do it for you. I decided on this for your benefit. If you're happy, I'm happy. Once I was content here on this farm. But since you came I've become unsettled, as if I were a mere boy."

"When would we go?"

"How about taking the Special Express on the thirtieth? The one they call the Peace Special. The Osaka station-master is a friend of mine, and I'll go in during the next two or three days and get the tickets from him."

These were not, however, the words Etsuko wanted to hear from Yakichi's lips. She had something different in mind, something so different as to freeze her heart, as she lay there ready to supplicate Yakichi's assistance. She regretted having extended him her throbbing hand earlier. Even with the bandage off, the pain of that hand seared her as if she were grasping hot coals.

"Before we go to Tokyo, there's something I wish you would do for me. While Saburo is away in Tenri, please fire Miyo."

"What a strange thing to ask!"

Yakichi was not entirely surprised. After all, is anyone surprised when a sick man asks for morning glories in the middle of the winter?

"What will you achieve by getting rid of Miyo?"

"Nothing, but I'm convinced she is the one who is causing me all this pain. Surely, no house would keep a maid around who was making the master sick, would it? Yet if things go on as they are, Miyo will kill me, I'm sure. If you don't get rid of her you will be indirectly responsible for my death. Which of us should go, then, she or I? If you want me to go, I'll take off for Osaka tomorrow and find a job."

"Stop it. Yet if I send Miyo away when she hasn't done anything, what will people say?"

"All right; then I'll leave. I don't want to stay here anyway."

"Then let's go to Tokyo, as I suggested."

"And you're going with me?"

Her words had in them little of tone or inflection, yet they had the power to make Yakichi imagine vividly what words they could be the preamble to. As if to forestall her saying those unsaid words, this old man in a checkered sleeping-kimono started edging over toward Etsuko's pallet.

Locked in the security of her quilt, Etsuko did not move. But two unwavering eyes directed themselves to meet Yakichi's gaze. They said nothing, those eyes, either of hatred or disgust—or love either—but they drove Yakichi back.

"No. No," she said, in low, impassive tones. "Until Miyo is told to go, it will be, 'No.' "

Where had Etsuko found the strength for this denial? Until this illness had come upon her, she had been accustomed to greet the approach of Yakichi's clumsy, worn-out machine by simply closing her eyes. Everything took place in the area around her—eyes tight-shut—on the periphery of her body. Even what took place upon her body was to her one of the events of the outside world. Where did her outer world begin? The inner world of this woman, capable of such delicate activity, was developing the captured, compressed, potential energy of an explosive.

For this reason Yakichi's confusion amused her.

"So you're being a coy damsel, are you? Very well. We'll give you your own way. While Saburo is away, turn Miyo out, if that's what you want. But—"

"But Saburo?"

"I don't think Saburo will take it."

"Saburo will leave," Etsuko said. "He'll go after Miyo, certainly. They're in love. In fact, letting Miyo go seems to me the only way to get rid of Saburo without firing him. It would be best for me if Saburo goes, but I don't want to be the one to tell him."

"At last we agree on something," said Yakichi.

At that moment the whistle of the last express departing from Okamachi station shattered the night air.

As Kensuke saw it, Etsuko's burn as well as her illness were just so much draft-dodging. "Take it from one who was one," he said, laughing. With Etsuko unavailable for help and Miyo—four months pregnant—unable to do heavy work, the burdens of weeding, harvesting the rice from the family's half-acre rice plot, digging potatoes, and bringing in the fruit crop all rested heavily on his shoulders. He went around as usual, incessantly muttering his discontent, shirking as much as working. Even this handkerchief-size plot of land, which had not been registered as a ricefield before the land reform, now had a delivery quota.

Saburo, his yearly participation in the Tenri Festival impending, worked with assiduity. The fruit crop was just about all garnered. In the intervals between crops he worked tirelessly, weeding, digging potatoes, and doing the autumn tilling. His labor under the clear autumn skies had tanned him further, turning him into a sturdy youth with a maturity that belied his years.

His close-cropped head seemed to have the solidity of that of a young bull. Not long before he had received a passionate love note from a village girl he barely knew and read it to Miyo with glee. He had received another note from another girl but had not mentioned it to Miyo. Not that he had anything to hide. Not that he wished to keep it a secret, or answer it and arrange a meeting with her. He simply kept quiet out of his own predilection for silence.

It was for him, however, a new experience. If Etsuko had so much as suspected that Saburo was aware that he was loved she would have considered it a momentous occurrence. He had become vaguely aware of the impression he made on the world around him. Until then he had considered that outer world not as a mirror but as just so much space through which he moved with perfect freedom.

This new experience had combined with the tan the autumn sun had brought to his cheek and forehead to bring out in his bearing a delicate, youthful arrogance he had never shown before. Miyo, her sensitivities heightened by love, saw it; but she interpreted it as a husbandly attitude directed toward her alone.

On the morning of October fifteenth Saburo set out, dressed in an old suitcoat given him by Yakichi, khaki trousers, the socks Etsuko had given him, and sneakers—his finest clothes. His luggage was a rough, canvas bookbag he carried slung from his shoulder.

"Speak to your mother about the wedding. Then, so that she can meet Miyo, have her come back with you. She can stay here for two or three days," said Etsuko. Even she was unaware why she was going over with him again this matter that was all settled. Was it because she considered these complications necessary so that she might force herself into an impossible situation? Was it because she wished to interrupt her plans by bringing herself to think about the terrible eventuality of having a mother come here and find the bride she had come to visit gone?

At any rate this was what she told Saburo quickly when she stopped him in the hall as he was on his way to Yakichi's room to say goodbye.

"All right. Thank you very much," said Saburo. His eyes gleamed with the restless energy of one setting out on a journey. His words of appreciation were somewhat exaggerated. He looked Etsuko full in the face—something he had never done before.

Etsuko wished to shake his hand, to feel the pressure of his callused palm. She started to thrust out her healing right hand, but decided that the burned surface would leave an unpleasant memory on his palm and held back. Saburo stood bewildered for a moment, flashed a cheerful parting smile, turned his back to her and hurried down the hall.

"That bag. My, it's small. One would think you were going to school," called Etsuko, behind him.

Miyo alone walked with him to the other side of the bridge. That was her right. Etsuko observed every detail of that right as she watched them go.

Where the gravel path ended at the steps leading down the hill, Saburo stopped, turned and saluted Yakichi and Etsuko standing in the yard. Long after his form had blended with the colored leaves of the *kaede* grove, the flash of his teeth, bared in a smile, shone in Etsuko's memory.

It was the hour for Miyo to set the rooms in order. In a matter of five minutes she reappeared, toiling languidly up the stone steps dappled with sunlight coming through the trees.

Etsuko needlessly said: "Saburo has gone, hasn't he?"

Miyo needlessly answered: "Yes, he's gone." Her face exhibited no sign either of joy or sadness.

Etsuko had watched Saburo depart with a heart gently, reflectively turbulent. Keen regret mingled with guilt feelings nagged at her. She toyed with the idea of wiping the slate clean by calling off the project of discharging Miyo.

She was provoked, however, by Miyo's face as she returned, already confidently settling down to her daily life with Saburo. Etsuko found herself smoothly slipping back into her original conviction that this project must not, by any means, be set aside.

5

"SABURO'S COMING! He's taking the shortcut across the ricefields over by the government housing. You can see him from upstairs. But he's alone—I don't see his mother!" Chieko had come running into the kitchen to inform Etsuko. It was the evening of the twenty-seventh, the day after the Tenri Festival.

Etsuko had been broiling mackerel on the small clay charcoal burner. She quickly moved the fish, along with the grill on which it had been broiling, to the counter nearby and placed the iron kettle over the coals. The simple serenity of her actions proclaimed the intensity of her emotions. She rose, gesturing to Chieko to accompany her upstairs.

The two women hurriedly climbed the stairs to the second floor. "That fellow Saburo really gets people excited here," said Kensuke, from the prone position he had assumed with his Anatole France novel. Shortly, however, he caught the mood of the women and came to stand beside them at the window.

The sun was half submerged in the wood west of the housing development. The sky glowed like a hearth.

The figure advancing across the stubbled fields was clearly Saburo, his pace firm, direction sure. Was there anything strange about this? This was the day; this was the time at which he had been expected all along.

His shadow stretched obliquely before him. He restrained the bag slung from his shoulder with one hand, as would a schoolboy, so that it did not swing. He wore no hat. His strong gait was filled with a repose that knew neither fear, nor apprehension, nor even fatigue. The route he was taking led to the highway. He swung right and took the raised path between the ricefields. Every once in a while he had to pick his way around the racks on which rice was drying.

Etsuko felt her heart beating wildly—from neither joy nor fear. She could not determine whether she was waiting for calamity or happiness, yet she knew that it had come—that which she awaited. The turmoil in her breast prevented her from saying what she knew she had to say. Somehow she managed to utter to Chieko: "What shall I do? I don't know what to do."

How surprised they would have been, Chieko and Kensuke, if they had heard these words from Etsuko a month earlier. She had changed. This once strong woman had lost her backbone. What she was looking forward to now was the last gentle smile Saburo would all unknowingly turn toward her, and the first terrible denunciation which—in the full knowledge he would have to come to—he would knowingly turn upon her. She was haunted by the memory of these past nights, filled with the turnings and returnings of those two anticipations.

What would happen thereafter seemed to her already established. Saburo would revile her; then he would set out after Miyo. At this time tomorrow Etsuko would no longer ever be able to see him. In fact, for all she knew, the last time she would ever be able to look at him to her heart's content would be here, from a distance, at this second-floor window.

"Don't be silly! Get hold of yourself!" said Chieko. "If you had the courage to fire Miyo, surely there's nothing you can't do. You really showed us. We admired you for it." She reached one arm around Etsuko's shoulder, as if encouraging a little sister.

To Etsuko the action of getting rid of Miyo had been her first attempt to ease her own suffering; it was also a concession, a surrender to that suffering. To Kensuke and his wife, however, it had looked like her opening attack.

To send a woman four months pregnant out of the house, wicker trunk on her back, is no small thing, reflected Chieko. Miyo's sobs, Etsuko's relentless determination, and the cold resolution with which she saw Miyo to the station and forced her onto the train—the melodrama which they had witnessed the day before—had moved Chieko and Kensuke mightily. They had never dreamed that such a performance would take place in Maidemmura. Her wicker trunk held to her back by a braided-palm cord, Miyo had descended the stairway, followed shortly by Etsuko looking like a constable.

Yakichi had shut himself up in his room and did not even look Miyo's way when she came in to say goodbye. "We appreciate your long service," was all he said. Asako, shocked speechless by these events, silently hovered about. Kensuke and Chieko, however, took pride in the fact that they needed not one word of explanation to know what was going on. These two flattered themselves into believing that they were capable of immorality because they were capable of comprehending immorality and vice—an attitude like that of newsmen assuming the pose of guardians of society.

"You've brought it off this far all alone; now we'll help you with the rest. Don't hesitate. We'll do whatever is in our power," said Kensuke.

"I'll do anything you say, Etsuko. What Father might think doesn't matter now," said Chieko.

The two vied with each other for Etsuko's attention as they looked out the window with her between them. Etsuko rose, started to brush back the hair at her temples and moved over to Chieko's mirror stand.

"May I use some of your cologne?"

"Do."

Etsuko took up the green bottle, sprinkled several drops in her hand and nervously applied it to her temples. The mirror was covered with a faded cover of Yuzen silk, which she did not remove. She was afraid to look at her face. Before long, however, she began to worry about how she would look to Saburo, whom she must meet in a few minutes. She pushed back the mirror cover. Her lipstick seemed too thick. She wiped her lips with a little lace-edged handkerchief.

How quickly we forget our actions! While the emotions in our memory linger, our actions pass without a trace. The Etsuko who had listened unmoved to the sobs of Miyo, unceremoniously and unfairly informed of her discharge; the Etsuko who had forced this poor pregnant girl to shoulder her belongings and then had practically prodded her onto the train—she found it hard to believe that that Etsuko and this Etsuko were the same woman. She felt no remorse; in fact she did not restrain the obduracy of her tense spirit in resisting remorse. She found herself perched helplessly on the series of agonies of her past, on the accumulated heap of her immobile, rotting emotions. Isn't the thing we call guilt the emotion that over and over brings men new lessons in lethargy?

Kensuke and his wife did not let this opportunity to help pass unnoticed. "If Saburo ends up hating you now, everything will be wasted. If only Father would say he was the one who fired Miyo! But, of course, he isn't big enough," said Chieko.

"He said that he wouldn't say anything to Saburo, that he was going to take no responsibility for it," said Etsuko.

"I don't blame him. Anyway, leave it to me. I won't do you any harm. What if I tell him that Miyo got a telegram saying her mother was sick, and she had to go off into the country and see her?" said Chieko.

Etsuko returned to herself. She saw this pair not as good counselors, but as two untrustworthy guides conducting her into a tepid, misty region she did not wish to enter. If she followed them, yesterday's determined actions would have no meaning.

Perhaps her act of firing Miyo had been nothing but a confession of her desperate love for Saburo. She preferred to think, however, that it was done for herself alone, so that she herself could live—an act which she could not avoid and which, therefore, she was justified in taking.

"Saburo must be given to understand clearly that it was I

who discharged Miyo. And I'll be the one to tell him. Please don't help me. I'll do it alone."

Kensuke and Chieko could only view Etsuko's cool resolve as wild-eyed determination born of desperation and bewilderment.

"Now look at it calmly. If you do what you say you'll ruin everything."

"Chieko's right; it isn't going to work. Just leave it to us. We won't harm you."

Etsuko smiled enigmatically and twisted her mouth slightly. She was arriving at the opinion that the only way she could remove the gratuitous obstacle this pair was placing in the way of her actions was to anger and alienate them. She slipped her hands back into her sash and adjusted it, and, like a great, weary bird listlessly adjusting its feathers, stood up. As she started down the stairs, she said: "You really needn't bother helping me. I'll get along."

Kensuke and Chieko were taken aback by Etsuko's rebuff. They were angry—with the anger that men wishing to help fight a fire might feel when restrained by the officer in charge. When it comes to controlling fires, the proper use of water is an absolute necessity, but this husband and wife were like the people who keep basins of lukewarm water ready to throw on fires.

"I wish I were able to turn away kindness like that," said Chieko.

"Incidentally," said Kensuke, "I wonder why Saburo's mother didn't come." They had been so involved with Etsuko's panic over the simple fact of Saburo's return that they had not even discussed this additional complication. The oversight irked Kensuke.

"Forget it. Just see if we help her anymore! It's a lot easier this way."

"Yes, we'll just relax and watch." Kensuke was himself at last. He regretted, nevertheless, that he had lost the sense of humane satisfaction that usually supported his taste for human misery.

Etsuko had returned to the charcoal burner, which rested on a counter Yakichi had installed by the veranda, where they cooked their meat and vegetables. She removed the iron kettle and replaced the grill.

With Miyo gone, the women had decided to take turns at cooking the rice. Today, the first day, it was Asako's turn. Nobuko was helping her by taking care of Natsuo. She was singing to him: their wild laughter echoed about the house, already thick with twilight.

"What's happening?" said Yakichi, coming out of his room and crouching down by the brazier. He nervously took up the cooking chopsticks and turned the fish.

"Saburo's come back."

"Is he here?"

"No, not quite."

The last traces of the setting sun clung to the leaves of the hedge of tea bushes that ran a few feet from the veranda. Tiny hard buds that had not yet flowered stuck out in a multitude of silhouettes. A branch or two protruding high out of the rather unkempt hedge shone gaily in the low rays of sun.

The sound of Saburo's whistle came up the stone stairs.

Etsuko recalled the tenseness of that time when Saburo had come to say goodnight and she, playing *go* with Yakichi, could not look his way. She dropped her eyes.

"Well, I'm back," called Saburo, standing on the other side of the hedge, which concealed his body below the chest. His shirt was open at the neck; his dark throat was bare. Etsuko's glance collided with his youthful, innocent grin. The thought that this would be the last time she would see his smiling face free of reproach imparted a painful intensity to her glance.

Yakichi grunted and bowed absently. He was looking at Etsuko, not Saburo.

The oil under the mackerel broke into flame. Etsuko did not move. Yakichi hurriedly blew it out.

"What is this? Here the whole house has seen more of Etsuko's love than it cares to, and this whippersnapper alone isn't aware of it," he said to himself.

With considerable annoyance, Yakichi again blew out flames that threatened to devour the fish.

Etsuko was now aware that she had deluded herself. She had bragged to Kensuke and Chieko that she would tell everything to Saburo, but now she saw clearly that her resolve was based on an imaginary courage. Having met this open, innocent, smiling face, how could she maintain that unlucky resolve? Yet now there was no one to whom she could turn for help.

Still, there had been in the courage Etsuko had paraded, even from the first, the fear that it would prove insufficient. Did it not contain, also, the fond hope that the hours of grace during which Saburo had not yet been told the truth, during which Etsuko could live under the same roof with him unhated by him, might ever be extended just a moment more?

After a time Yakichi said: "I don't understand. His mother isn't with him, is she?"

"No?" said Etsuko, with a question in her tone, as if she were noticing the fact for the first time. She felt uneasy, yet somehow happy: "Shall I go ask him if she is coming later on?"

"Forget it," muttered Yakichi; "if you do, you'll have to mention Miyo." The irony with which he cut off the discussion had the quality of aged, sagging skin.

For two days after that, Etsuko felt as if she was existing in the middle of an extraordinary calm. Those two days seemed like inexplicable, false symptoms of recovery occurring in someone hopelessly ill, ironic indications of a rally that ease the minds of his relatives and once again, however delusively, bring back hopes lost for a time.

What had happened? Was this happiness?

Etsuko took Maggie for a long walk. Then she went, with Maggie on her leash, to Okamachi station with Yakichi. He was going to Umeda terminal to make arrangements for the Special Express tickets. It was the afternoon of the twenty-ninth.

Three days earlier, she had gone, her face rigid, with Miyo to this same station. Now Yakichi stood there, leaning on the newly painted fence, chatting with her. He was dressed in a suit and carried a snakewood cane—he had even shaved. He let a number of Umeda-bound trains go by.

Etsuko was unusually cheerful, a fact that made Yakichi uneasy. She would scold the busily sniffing dog for rocking her off balance on her *geta*. Or she would gaze, smiling gently with slightly brimming eyes, at the people standing or passing by the bookstore and the butcher shop by the station. Red and yellow flags glistened in the advertisements of the children's magazines in the bookstore. It was a cloudy afternoon, with a cutting wind.

"I wonder if she's happy because she's been able to talk to Saburo," Yakichi mused. Maybe that's why she isn't coming to Osaka with me today. Yet, if so, I wonder why she hasn't objected to taking this long trip with me tomorrow."

Yakichi was mistaken. Etsuko's seeming happiness was the result of hours of pondering, which had brought her face to face with a vast enigma, which she was now quietly surveying with folded arms.

Yesterday Saburo had passed the day working in the fields as if nothing had happened. When Etsuko passed, he doffed his straw hat politely. This morning he had saluted her in the same way.

This quiet young man had nothing to say to his employers save as their orders or their questions required. He felt no discomfort when saying nothing all day. Were Miyo here, he would have been lively enough, all in fun. His resplendently youthful mien, even in silence, however, did not show the slightest trace of introspection or reserve. As if his whole body spoke, indeed sang, to nature, to the sun, every inch of him at work seemed brimming with the garrulity of life.

It even seemed possible to believe that deep in his simple, guileless spirit he was blithely confident that Miyo was still a member of this household and that, after the little business that kept her away was complete—perhaps even today—she would return. He might have felt a little uneasy about Miyo's absence, but he would never ask Yakichi or Etsuko where she was.

Etsuko liked to think that Saburo's demeanor was entirely attributable to her. After all, she had not told him what had happened to Miyo. Thus Saburo, naturally, had neither reviled her nor gone after Miyo. Etsuko's resolve to inform Saburo was weakening, though not only for her own sake. She was beginning to feel that she must do what she could to preserve this fleeting happiness she imagined she saw in Saburo.

But why his mother had not come back with him Etsuko was still at a loss to explain. Unfortunately, Saburo was simply not one to volunteer information about his trip and the events of the Tenri Festival.

Faint, inexpressible hopes—shadowy and imaginary, too ridiculous to articulate—came into being at the root of Etsuko's doubts. Torn between guilt and these hopes, she found that she dared not look Saburo in the face.

"That Saburo. Nothing bothers him. He looks as if he doesn't have a care in the world," Yakichi thought to himself as he stood in the station. "I figured, even Etsuko figured, that when we fired Miyo he would quit and go after her. But somehow we were wrong.

"But, what's the difference? When Etsuko and I go away, that will be the end of it. And when I get to Tokyo, who knows what good things may happen?"

Etsuko tied Maggie's chain to the fence and looked down the tracks. The rails gleamed in the cloud-wrapped day. Their dazzling steel surfaces, faceted with countless abrasions, seemed linked to Etsuko in undemonstrative, yet tender comradeship. From the blackened pebbles between the tracks traces of fine steel filings glinted. Soon the rails began to ring faintly, transmitting a distant vibration.

"I hope it doesn't rain," said Etsuko, abruptly. She thought of the trip she had taken to Osaka in September.

"Judging by this sky, it won't," said Yakichi, inspecting

the clouds. The ground shook as the Osaka-bound train came into the station.

"Are you ready to go?" said Etsuko.

"Why aren't you coming too?" insisted Yakichi, in a tone the noise of the train somehow justified.

"Look how I'm dressed. And there's the dog, too," said Etsuko lamely.

"We can leave Maggie at the bookstore. We've been buying there a long time, and they like dogs."

Etsuko thoughtfully untied the dog's leash. She was attracted to the notion of relinquishing this last half day in Maidemmura. To return home now to spend this evening with Saburo, as matters stood, suddenly seemed painful to her. She still found it difficult to believe that he was there, and that he had not left, never to be seen again, when he returned from Tenri a few days before. To make matters worse, he made her uneasy. Watching him in the field, swinging his mattock as if nothing mattered, filled her with fear.

Even the long walk she had taken the day before—had she not taken it in order to rid herself of that fear?

She unhooked the leash and said: "All right. I'll go."

Now here she was, in Osaka, where she had imagined she might end up when she had walked with Saburo down that untraveled highway. But now she walked with Yakichi. What strange events, what unexpected alterations, come into men's lives! Not until they were outside in the crowds did it occur to them that there was an underground passage leading to the Osaka terminal from the platform under the Hankyu store at which they had debarked.

Yakichi held his cane forward at an angle and, holding Etsuko's arm with his other hand, started across the intersection. Somehow they became separated.

"Hurry up! Hurry up!" he shouted at last, from the safety of the sidewalk on the other side.

They went halfway around the parking area, constantly menaced by blasts from the horns of passing cars, and were finally pushed into the turbulence of the Osaka terminal. A tough-looking young man was there, hawking tickets for the night train to anyone carrying luggage. Etsuko stared at this young ruffian, imagining how much his slender dark nape looked like Saburo's.

They crossed the great main floor, echoing with the noise of the loudspeaker announcing train departures and arrivals, and entered a hallway that seemed tranquil by contrast. Then they came to a sign reading: "Stationmaster."

While Yakichi talked to the stationmaster, Etsuko sat down in the anteroom, and there, ensconced in a white-linen-covered armchair, she unexpectedly dozed off. She was awakened by a loud voice shouting into a telephone. As she watched the station clerical personnel move about in the large office, she began to realize how exhausted she was. A great load of some kind oppressed her. Her weary heart felt pain simply from watching the violent motions of life. She sat there, her head pillowed in the chair back, watching the spectacle of a lone desk-top telephone drawing to itself now bell tones, now high chattering voices.

A telephone—it seems a long time since I last saw one. It's a strange device, constantly entangling the emotions of human beings within itself, yet capable of uttering nothing more than a simple bell tone. Doesn't it feel any pain from all the loves, the hatreds, and the desires that pass through it? Or is the sound of that bell really a scream of the pain, convulsive and unendurable, that the telephone continually inflicts?

"I'm sorry I was so long. I have the tickets, though. Seats on tomorrow's Special Express are very scarce. He was very kind."

Yakichi placed the two blue tickets in her outstretched hand. "They're second-class—just for you."

Actually, it was the third-class tickets that had been sold out. He could have purchased second-class tickets even at the windows. Once Yakichi set foot inside the stationmaster's office, however, he had to accept what was given him.

After that they went to the department store to buy some toothpaste, some toothbrushes, some vanishing cream for Etsuko, and some cheap whisky for the going-away party—if one could call it that—they were having this evening. Then they went home.

Their bags had been packed for tomorrow's trip since that morning. All Etsuko had to do, once she had packed the few items they had purchased in Osaka, was prepare the food—only slightly more elaborate than usual—for the party. Asako and Chieko (who had not been talking to Etsuko much of late) helped her in the kitchen.

Custom produces an almost superstitious way of observance. Thus Yakichi's decree that the whole family eat together in the unused ten-mat drawing room was not received with very good grace. "Etsuko," said Kensuke, in the kitchen, "it's strange that Father should ask that. It's almost as if you were going to Tokyo to stand by his deathbed. How good of you to take the trouble." He filched a piece of the food she was preparing.

Etsuko left to see whether the cleaning of the parlor was yet complete. In the faint glow of dusk, the unlighted room seemed as desolate as a great empty stable. Saburo was there alone sweeping, his face to the garden.

Perhaps it was the darkness of the room, or the broom in Saburo's hand, or the muffled sound of the broom gently brushing across the *tatami*, but the inexpressible loneliness of the young man there made a deep impression on Etsuko as she stood on the threshold observing. It was enough to make her believe she was seeing his inner self for the first time.

Guilt and passion alternately gnawed and burned her heart, each with equal intensity. As this new pain coursed through her, she felt the anguish of love as she had never before felt it. It must have been love that had made her feel since yesterday that she could not bear to look at him.

His loneliness, however, was to her a tangible, pure thing, which afforded almost no place for her glance to enter. Her lovesick longing trampled on memory, on reason; it even made Etsuko forget, little by little, the cause of the guilt she now experienced—Miyo. She would apologize only to Saburo; she would receive only his imprecations. In the very simplicity of her desire to punish herself appeared egoism in its purest form. Never before had this woman who seemed to think only of herself experienced an egoism so immaculate.

Saburo became conscious of Etsuko standing in the shadows and turned: "Was there something, ma'am?"

"You're just about done with the cleaning, aren't you?"

"Yes."

Etsuko advanced to the center of the room and looked around. Saburo stood still, the broom leaning against his shoulder. He was wearing a khaki shirt, its sleeves rolled up. Etsuko stood before him in the half-light like a wan ghost, her breast heaving.

"Oh," she said, with difficulty, "tonight, at one o'clock, will you meet me in the grape field in back? Before I go, there's something I must tell you."

Saburo said nothing.

"Well, will you come?"

"Yes, ma'am."

"Are you coming, or aren't you?"

"I'll be there."

"One o'clock. In the grape field. Don't let anyone know."

"Yes."

Saburo moved stiffly away, seemingly unaware of what he was doing.

The ten-mat room was fitted with a one hundred-watt bulb, but when it was turned on, there didn't even seem to be forty watts of light. Under this dim lamp, the parlor seemed darker than the evening gloom outside.

"My, it's depressing," said Kensuke. After that, for the rest of the meal, everyone took turns looking up at the bulb.

To make matters worse, they were eating from their most formal individual tables, arranged with Yakichi in the place of honor in front of the *tokonoma* and the other seven, counting Saburo, grouped around him in a semi-circle. In the forty-watt gloom, however, some of the small foods were so invisible that the appropriate U-shape grouping was, at Kensuke's suggestion, narrowed to permit greater light. This made the family look as if it were working indoors on the night shift instead of attending a party.

They toasted each other with the cheap whisky.

Etsuko was tormented by anxieties of her own making; Kensuke's clowning face, Chieko's incessant blue-stocking chatter, Natsuo's cheerful high-pitched laughter all made no impression on her. She was attracted, lured, by pain and uneasiness, much as a mountain climber is lured by ever higher ascents. She kept creating new anxieties, ever new agonies.

Nevertheless, there was in Etsuko's present uneasiness something tawdry, something quite different from the creative anxiety she had shown. When she had set out to get rid of Miyo signs of this new anxiety were already visible. It could lead to a succession of deliberate, monstrous miscalculations that could eventually deprive her of her allotted place on earth. It was as if she went out where other people came in—through a door as high as that of a fire lookout tower, to which many would never climb. Yet there Etsuko had resided all along, in a windowless room with a door she dared not open lest she plunge to her death. Perhaps the only basis, the only rationale, by which she could leave that room was the prior resolve that she would never depart from it.

She sat next to Yakichi, in a place that permitted her to go through the meal without seeing her aged traveling companion unless she turned to do so. Saburo, who sat directly across from her and who was having his glass filled by Kensuke, took up all her attention. His forthright, square hand seemed to nurse the glass, brimming with the liquor shining amber in the dim light.

It won't do at all for him to drink too much, Etsuko thought. *If he drinks too much, everything will be spoiled. He'll get drunk, go to sleep, and that will be that. I only have tonight, tomorrow I'll be on my way.*

When Kensuke tried to fill Saburo's glass again, Etsuko stretched out her hand.

"Now, don't be a picky old aunt. Let your darling boy have a drink." This was the first time Kensuke had ever mentioned Etsuko's feelings for Saburo before the assembled family.

Saburo clutched his empty glass and laughed. The import of Kensuke's words was lost on him. Etsuko smiled and calmly replied: "That stuff isn't good for young people." Then she quickly appropriated the bottle.

"Listen to Etsuko," said Chieko, taking her husband's side with restrained hostility; "she's the head of the Society for the Protection of Young People."

There was no real reason at this point that the taboo subject of Miyo's absence, now three days old, was not bandied about openly. Amazingly, just the right degree of hostility and just the right degree of kindness had worked to cancel each other out and maintain that taboo intact, a feat made possible by a tacit agreement involving Yakichi, who treated the entire matter as if he didn't know it existed; Kensuke and Chieko, whose kindness had been refused; and Asako, who didn't talk to Saburo. If however, just one clause of that agreement should be violated, there could be a crisis. It now seemed possible that Chieko would bring Etsuko's actions out in the open in her presence.

• • •

What will I do if, on this evening when I want to tell everything to Saburo and endure his recriminations, I should have to sit by while someone else tells him? He wouldn't show anger; he would just keep quiet, hiding his disappointment. Or, worse, he would be reticent with everyone present and smile as if to pardon me. And that would be the end of it all—of the pain I have anticipated, of my wild dreams, of my joyful annihilation. Nothing must happen until one o'clock in the morning! Nothing new is to come into existence until I do it myself!

Etsuko sat there without saying a word, her face drained of color.

It was Yakichi who came to her rescue. It was he, the unwilling and powerless sharer of her anxiety, who spoke up—he who, though only vaguely aware of the basis for Etsuko's concern, had had enough experience to measure the depth of her panic. And it was he who, for the sake of the next day's trip, rescued Etsuko from Kensuke and Chieko by launching into a long harangue filled with the party-killing propensities of the long-time company president.

"Yes, Saburo, you've had enough. When I was your age, now, I didn't smoke, much less drink. Now, you don't smoke, and that's admirable. When you're young, it pays not to have tastes you'll regret later on. Now when it comes to getting to like liquor, even forty isn't very late for that. It's even early for someone like Kensuke. Of course, times and generations differ. There is the difference between generations, and you have to keep that in mind, but just the same . . ."

There was a period of silence, interrupted by a burst of hysterical laughter from Asako. "Look," she said, "Natsuo's dropped right off. Let me just put him to bed."

She embraced the boy, who had fallen asleep on her lap, and stood up. Nobuko followed her out.

"Let's take a lesson from Natsuo and behave ourselves," said Kensuke, in a deliberately childish tone—aware of what Yakichi wished to achieve. "And, Etsuko, would you please give me the bottle back? I just want a drink for myself."

Etsuko had placed the bottle at her side, almost without realizing it; now, again barely conscious of what she was doing, she slid it over toward Kensuke.

She tried to look somewhere else than at Saburo but ended up looking only at him. He uncomfortably avoided her gaze.

As she gazed at Saburo, Etsuko thought of tomorrow's departure, which she had forced herself to consider inevitable. Now, however, that departure suddenly came to seem tentative, capable of alteration. The destination she was thinking about at that moment was not Tokyo, but—if one could call it a destination—the grape field behind the house.

The area the Sugimotos called the grape field was the section of their property once given over to grapes, occupied now by the peach orchard and the three abandoned greenhouses. It was the area through which they had walked on their way to view the cherry blossoms and to attend the festival, but outside of these occasions, the grape field was to the Sugimotos a spot seldom visited—a deserted island a quarter acre in size.

Etsuko could not keep from thinking about her preparations: how she would dress when she went to meet Saburo, how she would keep Yakichi from noticing her primping, what she would wear on her feet, how she would prop open the back door before retiring so that it would not creak and wake the household.

She realized that if what she wanted was a long talk with Saburo, she didn't need to go through all this secrecy, at an hour like that, at a place like that. It was really a laughable waste of effort. Were it now a few months back, when nobody was aware of her love, it would have been different. But that love was now practically an open secret, and if she wanted to avoid needless misunderstanding, she would have been better advised to schedule that meeting outside in broad daylight. Yet all she wanted was to make an abject confession, nothing more.

What was it that made her desire this elaborate secrecy? On this last night, Etsuko wanted her little secret, even if there was nothing to hide. It would be her first and perhaps her last secret with Saburo. She wanted to share it with him. Even if in the end he gave her nothing, she wished somehow to have him give her this trifling, not at all undangerous secret. She felt she had the right to ask this gift from him, whatever the cost.

From the middle of October on, Yakichi wore his knitted nightcap to bed to ward off the cold.

To Etsuko the nightcap had a strange significance. When he crawled into bed with it on his head, she knew she was not needed that evening. When he didn't wear it, she was wanted.

The going-away party had ended. It was eleven o'clock, and Etsuko could hear Yakichi breathing in sleep beside her. It is wise to get enough sleep the night before one takes a trip. His woolen nightcap had slipped to one side, exposing the ends of his oily white hair. His hair would never go snow-white; it would always be a rather untidy pepper-and-salt shade.

Etsuko looked at the black nightcap in the light of the floor lamp she used when reading in bed on nights she could not sleep. After a time she turned off the light. She did not want to have Yakichi open his eyes and get the impression that she was reading any later than usual.

She lay there in the dark and waited—almost two hours, an eternity of waiting. Her impatience and her feverish, unbridled imagination sketched the coming rendezvous with Saburo as something of limitless joy. The chore of confession by which she would bring Saburo's hatred down on herself was forgotten, like the prayers of a nun who, gripped by passion, has forgotten to pray.

Etsuko went into the kitchen and pulled the work dress she had concealed there over her nightgown. Then she tied a vermilion undersash around her waist, wrapped an old wool scarf the colors of the rainbow around her neck, and donned her black figured-satin coat. Maggie was sound asleep inside the dog house by the front door; there was no fear she would bark. Etsuko passed out the kitchen door and into the night, clear and bright as day beneath the moon.

She did not set out directly for the grape field, but instead walked over to Saburo's bedroom. His window was open. His bedclothes were thrown aside. He had swung out the window and preceded her to the grape field, of that there was no doubt. This evidence of his cooperation filled Etsuko's breast with an unexpected sensual thrill of joy.

The grape field, though usually loosely described as "in the back of the house," lay on the far side of a depression—practically a ravine—in which potatoes were grown. A bamboo thicket a few yards in depth ran along the edge of the grape field nearest the house, screening the greenhouses from view.

Etsuko passed through the potato gulley by a path deep in grass. She heard an owl call. The torn-up earth of the field, its potatoes already dug, loomed in the moonlight like a relief model of a mountain range fashioned of papier-mâché. Briers blocked one part of the path, beside which the prints of sneakers—Saburo's—showed for two or three paces in the loose earth.

She passed through the bamboos, climbed a small rise, and entered the shade of a *kashi* tree, from which she looked over a section of the grape field bright before her in the moonlight. In the doorway of the greenhouse, almost all its panes broken, stood Saburo, his arms folded, lost in thought.

The blackness of his close-cropped hair seemed to glow in the moonlight. He didn't seem to notice the cold; he wore no coat, but only a hand-knitted gray sweater handed down from Yakichi.

When he saw Etsuko, he dropped his arms smartly, brought his heels together, and bowed from the distance.

Etsuko approached, but she could not speak. She looked about for a moment and then said: "There's no place to sit down around here, is there?"

"Yes there is. In the greenhouse."

Etsuko was slightly disappointed that his tone was marked by not the slightest hint of hesitancy or shyness.

He bent his head and entered the greenhouse; she followed him. The frame of the practically glassless roof and the shapes of dried-up grape leaves were etched in shadows on the straw-strewn floor. A small, round, rain-washed wooden stool lay there. Saburo took out a handkerchief, wiped the stool carefully, and offered it to Etsuko. Then he tipped a rusty iron drum on its side and sat on it. He soon found it to be an unstable perch, however, and moved to the floor.

Etsuko said nothing. Saburo picked up a piece of straw and wound it around his fingers so that it squeaked.

The words gushed out of Etsuko's mouth: "I was the one who sent Miyo away."

"I know," said Saburo, looking up with perfect composure.

"Who told you?"

"Mrs. Asako told me."

"Asako?"

Saburo looked down. He rolled another straw around his fingers. He found it awkward to look at Etsuko in her consternation. To Etsuko's inflamed imagination the subdued demeanor of this boy with eyes downcast was part of his effort of the past few days at pretending to be happy in spite of the fact that he and his love had been so unreasonably separated. Now, after bearing this pain for so long, he still displayed this wholesome docility, this peerless gentility, behind which there lay only a wordless, indomitable resistance that wounded her more than the most violent imprecations. Her body coiled tightly on the stool.

She kept grasping one hand in the other as she spoke, pleading with him in a low, feverish voice. At times her speech was interrupted by what may well have been sobs, attesting to the strength of the emotions she was holding back. At times she seemed actually to be angry: "Please, forgive me. I was suffering terribly. There was nothing else I could do. Besides, you lied to me. You told me that you didn't love her, and all the while you and she were so much in love.

"How that lie made me suffer! I wanted to let you know the pain you were all unknowingly causing me, and felt I had to cause you to experience the same degree of unbearable agony. You can't imagine how much I suffered! I wish I could have taken that pain from my heart and placed it alongside the pain you are feeling now. Then we would know which is worse.

"I even lost control of myself and deliberately burned my hand in the fire. Look! I did it because of you. This burn was for you."

Etsuko held her hand out in the moonlight, exposing the burn. Saburo reached out his hand, touched Etsuko's fingertips as if he were touching something horrible, and quickly let go.

"At Tenri, I saw beggars like this. Beggars show you their wounds to make you sorry for them. They're horrible. And yet the madam is like some kind of proud beggar," he said to himself.

This was as far as Saburo's thoughts went. He did not know it was Etsuko's pain that made her proud.

He still did not know that Etsuko loved him.

He strained to grasp in Etsuko's rambling confession that

kernel of truth he could understand. This woman was suffering. That much was certain. She was suffering, and though he couldn't fathom why he knew that the reason was connected with him. When someone is suffering, you have to do what you can to make him feel better. If only he knew how . . .

"It's all right. You don't need to worry about me. Without Miyo around, it's a little lonely once in a while, but that's no great matter," he said.

Etsuko could not believe he was telling the whole truth. She was dumbfounded by the extraordinary magnanimity he was displaying. Her highly skeptical glance was directed at finding, inside his simple, gentle sympathy, the self-abasing lie, the reserved decorum.

"You're still not telling me the truth. The one you love has been forcibly dragged off, and you say it's no great matter? How can that be? Here I'm telling you all this, apologizing to you, and you still refuse to come out and tell me how you really feel. Can't you bring yourself to forgive me?"

In Saburo's simple, transparent soul, there lay no defense, however unavailing, against this nebulous, romantic *idée fixe* held by Etsuko. He didn't know where to begin. It seemed to him, however, that what she was basically concerned about was his lie, the great lie that she had just attacked: "I don't love Miyo." If he could somehow convince her that statement was true, surely she would feel better.

He pronounced his next words with great care: "It is not a lie. You really do not need to worry about me, madam, because I do not love Miyo."

Etsuko was almost laughing—she certainly was not crying: "Again you lie! Again the same lie! Do you really think you're going to fool me with a childish fib like that?"

Saburo did not know what to say. Before this woman with whom his words had no effect, he was completely without recourse. There was nothing to do but keep silent.

For the first time, Etsuko found herself relaxing in the presence of his gentle wordlessness. The sound of the whistle of a distant freight train flying through the deep night pierced her ears.

Saburo, deep in thought did not even hear it . . . "What can I tell her so she'll believe me? Last time she went on about this 'Love, don't love' business as if it were going to turn the world upside down. Yet, now, she won't accept anything I say, telling me it's a lie. All right, it seems she needs proof. If I tell her the whole truth, she'll believe me," he thought.

He moved into a half-crouching position and launched into a narrative: "It's no lie. I never wanted much to have Miyo for my wife. In fact, I talked to Mother about that at Tenri. She's against it. 'It's too early for you to get married,' she says. I barely had the nerve to tell her that Miyo's going to have a baby. Then Mother got even more against it. 'Why do I want to take a stupid girl like that for a daughter-in-law?' she says. 'I don't even want to see the face of a nasty girl like that.' So she didn't come to Maidemmura, and went straight home from Tenri."

This artless tale, so haltingly recounted, brimmed with an elusive honesty. Etsuko abandoned herself to the intense joy, the dreamlike ecstasy of this fleeting moment. As she listened, her eyes gleamed, her nostrils quivered.

As if deep in a trance she said: "Why didn't you tell me? Why didn't you tell me this right away?"

Then she went on in the same way: "Of course . . . that's why your mother didn't come back with you."

Then she went on in the same way: "At that rate, when you got back here and Miyo wasn't here, it worked out perfectly, didn't it?"

Her words were half thought, half spoken. She had difficulty distinguishing between the soliloquy that kept insistently repeating itself in her mind and the soliloquy that she uttered.

In dreams, seedlings mature instantly into fruit-bearing trees, and small birds become winged horses. So in Etsuko's trance, outlandish hopes waxed into the shape of hopes capable of immediate realization.

What if I am the one Saburo has loved? I will have to be bold and try to find out. I must not even think that what I anticipate will not come true. If my hopes come true, I shall be happy! It's that simple.

Thus Etsuko pondered. Hopes for whose fruition one does not fear, however, are not hopes so much as, in the last analysis, a species of desperation.

"All right; but, then, who in the world do you love?" Etsuko asked.

Surely this sagacious woman was making a mistake here, for in these circumstances it was not words that would bring her and Saburo together. If she but reached out her hand and gently touched Saburo's shoulder, perhaps everything might have begun. Just the intermingling of hands, perhaps, would have served to fuse these two disparate spirits together.

But words stood between them like an intransigent ghost, so Saburo did not interpret as he should have the blood that flooded Etsuko's cheeks. He was like a child face to face with a difficult problem in algebra. The only answer he had was retreat.

"Love . . . don't love—not again! No, not again," he said to himself.

This counter-word, *love*, at first glance so convenient, had brought an excess of meanings into the life he had been leading with so little reflection. It promised, furthermore, to impose unnecessary structuring on the life he would live in the future. He could not think of it as representing anything more than a completely unnecessary concept.

He found no room in his life fitted out for this word as a daily necessity, as something for which he would at times place his life in the balance. It was difficult for him even to imagine it. And the stupidity that leads some owners of such a room to burn the whole house down in order to rid themselves of it was to him utterly ridiculous.

A young man stood beside a young woman. It was entirely natural that Saburo should kiss Miyo. They copulated. And thus a child sprouted in Miyo's womb. And then it was entirely natural that Saburo should tire of Miyo. Their childish play had reached its peak, and he no longer needed Miyo for that play; anyone would do just as well. In fact, saying he tired of Miyo may not be correct. To Saburo, Miyo no longer had to be Miyo; that was all.

Saburo never acted by the proposition that if a person did not love someone he would have to be in love with someone else, or that if he loved someone he could not be in love with someone else. Again, therefore, he couldn't answer her.

• • •

Who was it that was pushing this innocent boy into a corner in this way? Who was to blame for pushing him into a corner and making him give ill-considered answers?

Saburo decided that he must depend not on his own inclinations but on a practical, worldly tactic—a course that is common enough among men who have dined since childhood on the food of strangers.

Once he had made this decision, it did not take him long to read in Etsuko's eyes the wish that he speak her name.

"Her eyes are wet with concern, aren't they? That's it. The right answer is her name; that's what she wants. No doubt about it," he thought.

He picked one of the wrinkled grapes near him and rolled it in his hand. Then he looked down and said, succinctly: "Madam, it's you."

The lie in his tone was only too obvious. It said "I do not love you" more unequivocally than the words "I do not love you" would have. No cool head was necessary to see through his artless lie. Even Etsuko, therefore, deep in her trance though she had been, came to herself with his words.

It was all over.

She put her hands back and adjusted her hair, cold from the night air. Then she said, in a composed, rather heroic tone: "We'd better get back. We have to leave early tomorrow, and I'd better get a little sleep, anyway."

Saburo dropped his left shoulder slightly and stood up, rather disconsolately. Etsuko felt cold at her neck and adjusted her scarf. Saburo noticed that her lips shone dark in the shadow of the withered grape leaves.

Saburo was weary of this tedious dialogue. What caught his eye as he looked up now and again was not a woman, but some kind of spiritual monster, some undefinable spiritual embodiment—hating, suffering, bleeding, or raising a shout of joy—pure raw nerves incarnate.

As she stood up, however, her scarf close about her neck, Saburo became conscious for the first time that she was a woman. As she started to leave the greenhouse, he extended his arm and barred her way.

Etsuko twisted her body and stared at him as if to stab him into desisting. As a boat propelled through water thick with weeds has its oar strike the bottom of another boat, so the firm flesh of his arm, in spite of the layers of clothing intervening, collided palpably with the soft flesh of her breasts.

He was not deterred at all by her stare. He opened his mouth gently. Then he chuckled reassuringly, without a sound. Then, seemingly without realizing it, he blinked rapidly two or three times.

Why did Etsuko say nothing all this time? Was it because she had finally come to understand that words were useless? Was it because, like a man who looks down at the bottom of a precipice and becomes fascinated by it until he can think of nothing else, she had at last grasped the failure of her hopes and now could not let go?

Pressed here by this joyful, heedless young flesh, she started to perspire. One of her *zori* came off and slid away upside-down.

She resisted, without knowing why. She resisted—as if she were leaning against something.

He held her firmly, both her arms pinioned to her sides. She kept moving her head so that their lips never met. In the intensity of the struggle, Saburo tripped over the stool and fell to one knee in the straw. Etsuko slipped from his arms and dashed from the greenhouse.

Why did she scream? Why did she call for help? Whom did she call? What name was there other than *Saburo* that she would want to call that much? Where was there anyone to rescue her other than Saburo? So why did she call for help? And what would it achieve? Where was she . . . where would she go . . . where was she to be rescued from and where was she to be taken?

Saburo ran after her and threw her down into the pampas grass that grew rankly by the greenhouses. Her body fell deep into a clump of vegetation. The weeds cut their hands, mixing blood with the sweat upon them, of which they were unaware.

Etsuko saw Saburo's face close to hers, red, sweaty and shining. She thought: *Is there anything in this world so beautiful as a young man's countenance made beautiful by lust, radiant by passion?* Detached from these thoughts, her body still resisted.

Saburo held the woman down with the force of his chest and his arms and, at the same time, as if he were playing, bit the buttons loose from her black satin coat. Etsuko was only half conscious. She felt only a bursting affection for this great, heavy, active head rolling about on her breast.

Yet in that moment she screamed.

Before Saburo could be surprised by that piercing scream, his lithe body recovered its faculties and prepared to flee. Not out of logic, nor any conditioned emotional response—flight came into his mind by the very same process of direct apprehension that occurs in animals whose lives are in danger. He withdrew his body, stood up and started in the direction away from the Sugimoto home.

A terrible power came into being in Etsuko. She sprang out of the half-stupor in which she had been sunk, and grasped the retreating Saburo.

"Wait! Wait!" she screamed.

The more she commanded, the more he retreated. As he fled, he attempted to free his body from the restraining arms of the woman. She clung to his thigh with all her power, barely realizing she was being dragged through briers.

Yakichi opened his eyes and saw that Etsuko was not on the pallet beside him. Feeling his worst fears justified, he went to Saburo's room, where he found another empty bed. In the soil outside the window he saw footprints.

He returned to the kitchen and saw the back door standing open in the moonlight. If they had gone out this way, he surmised, surely they were headed for the pear orchard or the grape field. He had been working daily in the pear orchard, however, and knew its soil was freshly turned. He took the path to the grape field.

He started down the path, but suddenly stopped and turned. In the doorway of the shed stood a mattock. He grasped the handle and took the tool with him—not for any deep reason; for defense, perhaps.

As he came to the edge of the bamboo thicket, Yakichi heard Etsuko screaming. He shouldered the mattock and started to run.

As Saburo struggled desperately to escape, he turned and saw Yakichi running toward him. His legs refused to move. He stood still and watched Yakichi, fiercely panting, run up to him.

Etsuko felt the power go out of Saburo's efforts to escape and stood up wondering what had happened. Her body should have been one mass of pain, but she was not aware of it. She realized that someone was standing beside her. It was Yakichi in his nightclothes. He stood with the mattock resting at his side. His chest protruded naked from his sleeping kimono, laboring with his tortured breath.

She looked him in the eye without wavering.

The old man's body was quivering all over. He looked down, unable to meet her gaze.

His irresoluteness filled her with anger. She seized the mattock from the old man and swung it at Saburo's shoulder. He was standing beside her in shock, awaiting nothing, comprehending nothing. The well-honed white steel passed above his shoulder and cut through the nape of his neck.

The young man emitted a small, suppressed shout from somewhere in the vicinity of his throat and tottered forward. The next blow slashed him across the skull. He put his hands to his head and fell.

Yakichi and Etsuko stood rooted, watching the still faintly writhing body. Actually, they saw nothing at all.

After a number of seemingly endless, wordless seconds, Yakichi spoke: "Why did you kill him?"

"Because you didn't."

"I wasn't planning to kill him."

Etsuko turned toward him with a mad stare: "You're lying. You were going to kill him. That's what I was waiting for. You couldn't save me without killing Saburo. Yet you hesitated. Standing there shaking. Shamelessly shaking. So I had to kill him for you."

"You can't lay the blame on me!"

"Who is? Tomorrow morning early, I'll go to the police. I alone."

"Take your time. There are a lot of things that must be thought through. But why, oh why, did you have to kill him?"

"He was making me suffer, that's why."

"But it wasn't his fault."

"Not his fault? That's not so. He got what he deserved for hurting me. Nobody has the right to cause me pain. Nobody can get away with that."

"Who is to say they can't?"

"I say so. And what I say, no one can change."

"You're a terrifying woman."

Yakichi breathed a long sigh, as if discovering for the first time that he was not the perpetrator of the crime: "Listen. Let's take our time. We can take our time and decide what to do. Until then, though, we'd better make sure no one finds him."

He took the mattock from Etsuko's hand. The handle was wet with spattered blood.

Yakichi's next task was a strange one. Nearby was a plot of land prepared for upland rice planting. There, like a man cultivating far into the night, he assiduously set to digging a hole.

During the fairly long period it took Yakichi to dig the shallow grave, Etsuko sat on the ground staring at Saburo's body, face down. His sweater was pulled up slightly, and the bare skin of his back showed where his khaki shirt had ridden up with the sweater. That skin showed forth an ashen earth color. One cheek was pressed deep into the sod; from his mouth, twisted from pain, protruded a row of sharp white teeth. He almost seemed to be smiling. Beneath his forehead, oozing with brain matter, his eyelids seemed sunk in, they were closed so tightly.

Yakichi finished digging, went to Etsuko's side, and tapped her lightly on the shoulder.

The head and trunk were bloody and hard to grasp, so Yakichi took the corpse by the legs and dragged it across the grass. Even in the dark, black spots were visible where he had lain. Saburo's upturned face and head shook as if nodding as it struck stones or thick clods of the earth.

Yakichi and Etsuko quickly threw dirt on the corpse stretched out in the shallow grave. At last all that remained was the smiling face, eyes closed and mouth half open. The front teeth shone stark white in the moonlight. Etsuko threw down the mattock, scooped up some dirt with her hand and sprinkled it into the mouth. Dirt rained into that dark cave of a mouth. Yakichi raked in a great mass of soil from the side of the hole with the mattock and covered the dead face.

When the corpse was covered thickly with dirt, Etsuko walked on it, wearing only her *tabi*, to pack it down. The soft soil felt familiar—as if she were walking on bare skin.

In the meantime Yakichi walked about, inspecting the ground and trampling out bloodstains. After that he covered them with dirt, which he trampled again and scattered.

• • •

In the kitchen, they washed the soil and the blood from their hands. Etsuko took off her *tabi* and her coat, which had been sprayed with blood. She had found her *zori* and worn them on the walk back.

Yakichi's hands were shaking so severely he couldn't dip up water. Etsuko, who was not shaking at all, dipped it for them. She carefully wiped away the bloodstains that had formed in the sink.

Etsuko left first, carrying her coat and *tabi*, rolled in a ball. She barely felt the skinburns and bruises she had suffered when dragged by Saburo. That was not true pain anyway.

Maggie howled, then suddenly stopped.

What can compare with the sleep that came upon Etsuko like divine favor as soon as she slipped into bed? Yakichi listened in amazement to her peaceful breathing. Extended fatigue, endless fatigue, tremendous fatigue far more immeasurable than the crime Etsuko had just committed, fulfilling fatigue derived from countless pains accumulated in the process of performing some efficacious act—surely no one could acquire innocent sleep like this without having paid for it with fatigue like that?

Nevertheless, after the short period of rest that had been vouchsafed to her, Etsuko awoke. Around her lay deep darkness. The wall clock chopped out the heavy, melancholy seconds, one by one. Beside her Yakichi lay, sleepless and shivering. Etsuko did not speak. No one would hear her voice. She deliberately opened her eyes to the darkness in the room. She could see nothing.

She could hear a distant cockcrow. Even now, with the dawn still distant, the roosters were crowing back and forth.

Far away—where, she could not tell—one crowed. Then another, as if to answer the first. Then another. Then another. The crowing of roosters in the middle of the night, fittingly, knows no end. It went on again. It went on beyond ending.

. . . yet, there wasn't a thing.

BOOKS BY YUKIO MISHIMA

SPRING SNOW

The first novel of Mishima's tetralogy, *The Sea of Fertility*, is set in Tokyo in 1912, when the hermetic world of ancient aristocracy is being breached for the first time by outsiders—rich provincial families unburdened by tradition, whose money and vitality make them formidable contenders for social and political power.

Fiction/Literature/0-679-72241-6

RUNAWAY HORSES

The second novel of the tetralogy is the chronicle of a conspiracy, a novel about the roots and nature of Japanese fanaticism in the years that led to the war—an era marked by economic depression, the upheaval of radical social change, political violence, and assassination.

Fiction/Literature/0-679-72240-8

THE TEMPLE OF DAWN

In this third novel of the tetralogy, the story of one man's obsessive pursuit of a beautiful woman and his equally passionate search for enlightenment, Mishima powerfully dramatizes the Japanese experience from the eve of World War II through the postwar era.

Fiction/Literature/0-679-72242-4

THE DECAY OF THE ANGEL

As the dramatic climax of *The Sea of Fertility* tetrology, this novel brings together the dominant themes of the three previous novels: the meaning and decay of Japan's courtly tradition and samurai ideal; the essence and value of Buddhist philosophy and aesthetics; and, underlying all, Mishima's apocalyptic vision of the modern era, which saw dissolution of the moral and cultural forces that throughout the ages nourished a people and a world.

Fiction/Literature/0-679-72243-2

THE SAILOR WHO FELL FROM GRACE WITH THE SEA

Mishima tells of a band of savage thirteen-year-old boys who reject the adult world as illusory, hypocritical, and sentimental, and train themselves in a brutal callousness they call "objectivity." When the mother of one of them begins an affair with a ship's officer, her son and his friends idealize the man at first; but it is not long before they conclude that he is in fact soft and romantic. They regard their disappointment in him as an act of betrayal on his part, and react violently.

Fiction/Literature/0-679-75015-0

THE SOUND OF WAVES

Set in a remote fishing village in Japan, this is a timeless story of first love. It tells of Shinji, a young fisherman, and Hatsue, the beautiful daughter of the wealthiest man in the village. Shinji is entranced at the sight of Hatsue in the twilight on the beach, where she has been training to be a pearl diver. They fall in love, but must endure the calumny and gossip of the villagers.

Fiction/Literature/0-679-75268-4

THE TEMPLE OF THE GOLDEN PAVILION

Because of the boyhood trauma of seeing his mother make love to another man in the presence of his dying father, Mizoguchi becomes a hopeless stutterer. Taunted by his schoolmates, he feels utterly alone until he becomes an acolyte at a famous temple in Kyoto, where he becomes obsessed with the temple's beauty. In the novel's soaring climax, he tries desperately to free himself from his fixation.

Fiction/Literature/0-679-75270-6

Printed in the United States
by Baker & Taylor Publisher Services